TIM HARTWELL
and the Brutus of Troy

Aeneas Middleton

TIM HARTWELL and The Brutus of Troy

Royal Middleton publishing
New York, NY
royalmiddletonpublishing@gmail.com

ISBN-13: 978-0615600093
ISBN-10: 0615600093

Library of Congress Control Number: 2012902303

Middleton, Aeneas, 1980-
Tim Hartwell and The Brutus of Troy: by Aeneas Middleton
–
1st Edition | Series 1
Book Two (Bk. 2)
Edited by Ruth Goodman

Printed in the United States of America

Cover and book design by Aeneas Middleton

Troïa Nova

-New Troy-

Approx. 1103 BC

N
W · E
S

Brutus' Palace

Temple
Of Diana
(Stone Of Brutus
/London stone)

THAMES

RIVER

TIM HARTWELL series

Tim Hartwell and The Magical Galon of Wales (Book One)

Tim Hartwell and The Brutus of Troy (Book Two)

*Tim Hartwell and The Death of Ages (Book Three)

*TBA (Book Four)

*TBA (Book Five)

*TBA (Book Six)

*TBA (Book Seven)

*TBA (Book Eight)

*TBA (Book Nine)

[*Coming soon]

Contents

6   Mountains of Red Rock

20   War on Glyder Fawr

38   Funeral Games in Troia Nova

99   Battle on the River Thames

118   Revenge Is Bittersweet

135   Meeting with Claudius

180   Down the Hoist

195   The Gates of Death

210   Coat of Arms / Map / Brutus

Mountains of Red Rock

Cumulonimbus grey clouds begin to clear Crib Goch above. Lancer leads the pack out of the patch of mist down to Lyn Lydaw. They all notice Brutus of Troy sitting on his powerful horse. As he rides closer, they see the horse's muscular legs and beautiful dark-brown solid color coat glowing.

God's rays shine through a patch of cumulus clouds high above them in the sky. Brutus has mid-length hair. His skin is golden from the sun, and the sun bounces off his armored chest plate. The chest plate sparkles in every direction, almost blinding Tim as Ceri pulls down her hood to block the shine reaching inside part of her hood. Brutus jumps off his horse, sticking his sword into the ground as the sword sways from left to right. Lancer nods then calls out the name of a Trojan legend.

"Brutus, Brutus of Troy. We thank you for coming at this special time of need, for we know you are headed to fulfill more of your destiny. We are anxious to see what you can teach young Mr. Hartwell, for he is the chosen one, the boy who carries the Book of Hartwell and the magical power of the Galon," Lancer says firmly.

Lancer places his hand on Brutus' shoulder, noticing that he has a cloth wrapped around his left wrist, embroidered with patterns of ancient Troy. Brutus gives his comrade a proper handshake then walks over to Ceri, placing his hand over the top of the hood on her cloak.

"I see Ceri remains unknown to the earth. I truly respect that, little one. Even though, how can you see your opponent if he is right behind you?" Brutus asks politely.

"It doesn't take much effort most of the time. All you have to do is this." Ceri jumps into the air, pulling down Verlock and Alfred (the sneaky twin Wyvern gargoyles) who both thought they were invisible. Ceri lands back on the ground as the Wyverns' invisibility spell wears off.

"How . . . how did you know we were here?" Alfred and Verlock ask Ceri with their necks still trapped in her arm.

"I've always heard the sound of Wyvern blood flowing through their veins," Ceri says to Brutus who is astonished with her magical ability. Then he dusts off his shoulder while getting back to the urgent business at hand.

"Lancer and Ceri, we don't have time to waste. Tim must begin his training immediately, for my time here isn't long."

The group begins to move out, leaving Verlock and Alfred behind. Three horses come toward them on the horizon, moving as fast as the wind. They ride directly up to Lancer, Ceri, and Tim and stop in front of them so they can hop on. Each horse has the Hartwell coat of arms cloth dangling from its side, which was supplied by Verlock and his twin brother Alfred.

Time passes, then the air begins to have more mist than ever as Lancer, Ceri, and Tim reach the west peak of the Nantlle Ridge inside Craig Cwm Silyn.

"Some of the most notable crags are here," says Brutus. "This location has been used over time to train the best. Even my three sons were trained here by me. My oldest, Locrinus, loved it the most." Brutus smirks as he gets off his horse, looking at the rock formations sticking out of the ground every which way. He walks over to one of the rocks, touching it with his right hand as rain begins to drizzle from all angles. Brutus' magical horse snorts near the rock slab right next to them.

"I feel it too," Brutus says as Tim looks

over toward the horse moving its front legs in a weird pattern.

"Your horse was always special, Brutus," Lancer says proudly as Brutus reaches down toward the ground, looking at the dirt.

"Ceri and Lancer, head to my palace in Troia Nova," says Brutus. "After we are done here, we will meet you there for a feast, my friend Lancer. It was a please to see yo again." He adds.

Lancer and Ceri turn their horses around and ride off toward Troia Nova, leaving Brutus and Tim at the Mynydd Graig Goch for Tim's training, which can be deadly to anyone up for the challenge.

Brutus quickly snaps his fingers, which shrinks them both to the size of microscopic insects. The rocks, which now seem large, are the size of Snowdon Mountain. The lights come from afar since Brutus and Tim are small enough to fit under a human fingernail. The tors of rock sitting on the summit tower are jagged, and the wind is much stronger than before. Brutus starts to speak as he unsheathes his sword, suspicious of what is about to come as the rain begins to pour harder from above.

"We must make it to the top of this summit. There will be a light source at the highest point, which you have to touch to end your training. You could lose your life at anytime. No time to run from the tiger beetle which are taller than the highest tree, faster than a snake's head, and they have powerful jaws. My other son, Kamber, was almost killed by one of these God-made creatures. Keep your eyes open, Tim, and let us get there at once. You have to touch the light so we can both travel through it to get back to Troia Nova."

Brutus continues to explain the nature of the training. Tim remains confident as he walks from under one of the rocks that appears to be the height of a skyscraper in modern London. Brutus grabs Tim's shirt, pulling him back as an army of tiger beetles run past their location. Tim and Brutus fly back, as both of them were almost killed. The ground rumbles as if there's an earthquake, and the beetles' legs bash down, trampling over each other with their green-shell exoskeletons. An army of tiger beetles covers the sky. Some of the light flashes in the crack of the rock; the tiger beetles move past the rock that Brutus and Tim are standing directly under.

Hundreds of ultrasonic clicks from the beetles fill the air, one after another. The beetles disappear, allowing light to come back down from the sky. Distant sounds of them moving fill the air from other locations. It is a sound that cannot be mistaken. Brutus tells Tim to run behind him as he dashes over to another mountain rock and slides through a crack between two crags. Brutus looks around, trying to stay out of the sight of the creatures that stalk the land. Even the wind can easily sweep both Brutus and Tim off their feet.

Brutus is not afraid, and Tim keeps plenty of courage around to fulfill his destiny. He can feel the rain as it pours harder, making the earth seem like it's under a waterfall. Hanging on for his life, Tim wonders what events are ahead.

"Come on!" Brutus shouts, for the magical power of the Galon has briefly taken over Tim's emotions. The Trojan commander looks to the right, for he doesn't hear any sound from the tiger beetles, which usually means they are in full attack mode under the power of Selwyn's Chancer. Brutus and Tim wait for the perfect time to move. Tim dashes toward the next rock as a huge tiger beetle jumps out of nowhere, its legs slamming on the summit behind Tim. Brutus slides underneath a rock, protecting himself from the jaws of beetle that crept behind him. Brutus looks back at Tim, wondering if he has enough courage to follow him. Brutus yells out "Firewyn," which ignites the sacred blue flame on Tim's arms.

Tim shoots huge projectiles of light and fire toward the beetle in front of him. The fire twirls around the beetle, slashing it like a knife and burning it alive at the same time. Brutus looks on with amazement, never having seen anyone so powerful, except the gods. The 4th Galon appears around Tim's neck and sends a magical light from the sky, blinding the beetle. Tim jumps into a lake under the beetle, which, at human size, would be the size of a raindrop. Getting back together safely, Brutus and Tim continue to run toward the peak of the large rocky summit.

Out of nowhere, thousands of tiger

beetles begin storming toward them. Dashing as fast as he can, Tim begins burning some of the beetles, which fall to earth and send shock waves throughout the summit. Brutus and Tim run with all their might, jumping between another gorge, which seems more like a small cave to them. The beetles are too big to enter, as thousands of them try to get inside the crack. Even with their size, the rock's density is too strong for something so titan-like.

With no possible way to escape without being chewed alive, Brutus begins to tell Tim that he must survive. The training regime has changed, for Brutus has never seen the beetles ready to murder anything in sight before.

"I'm surprised we are both alive,"

Tim says, and adds some humor. Brutus says nothing but whispers a few things about Lancer, informing him of the power of Stratford Hartwell and his parallel world of Selwyn's Chancer.

The beetles disperse as the darkness transforms into light. The towering beetles leave fast as the sun begins to shine through, giving warmth to their skin.

Brutus quickly yells, "It's time to run!" He dashes across the ground, heading under rock after rock and even between them. Brutus and Tim continue to move up long paths of narrow rocks to an opening where mist flows toward the center of the opening of the path. Another light-yellow light source begins to glow in a gap directly in front of them. Tim turns off his Firewyn spell, leaving the flame to fade out over his arms. He takes a deep breath and runs to the light. As he touches it, Tim magically opens a doorway. It's the Stairwell of Travel to Troia Nova. Brutus and Tim, without hesitation, jump into the light, hoping for a conclusion to this training madness. Brutus now knows the power of the Galon has changed inside Selwyn's Chancer forever.

War on Glyder Fawr

The sky is a dark pastel blue, and clouds are drifting across the earth's troposphere. Below the clouds on the ground are Lancer and Ceri, riding through Lyn Lydaw as the air remains brisk with mist moving along the ground. Lancer wraps his scarf around his nose and mouth, dusting off some of the dirt that flew on him. They begin to ride up to Glyder Fawr. Without hesitation, thousands of red flames appear in the sky, almost like comets going across the horizon, as the flaming light gets closer and closer. Ceri looks up at millions of Diablo Archwings flying between Glyder Fach and Y Garn. The secondary fleet of Diablo Arches travel by land near a river as far as Lancer and Ceri can see off the horizon.

Lightning strikes throughout the dark night. Ceri senses trouble, so she yells over to Lancer to head for the rocky outcrop directly ahead of them. The fire-lit black arrows fly closer to them from the sky. Lancer puts on his mask and quickly says to Ceri, "You can only hear the arrows within one meter. Some of the House of Diablo Arches ride their black horses, which stomp the ground, for war has been declared on the few remaining royal descendants of the House of Gwynwell."

Ceri jumps behind one of the many spiky rocks. Lancer does the same, just in time for one of the Diablo arrows to fly past Lancer's head, scratching off some of the gold trim on his helmet.

"Most of them explode like a hand-sized atomic bomb. You're lucky," Ceri says to Lancer as she places her hand on the rock, sending a light-green electric current through the rocks around them. The current joins into one gigantic stream of electric current, leading all the way up to the dark-blue stratosphere.

The power Ceri has summoned brings a titan, amber-colored dragon wearing a V-neck collar with the House of Trydan on the front of it. The Trydan dragon is made from pure energy that thrives inside them. This royal species evolved throughout the ages of Selwyn's Chancer. Not even Stratford could believe a new species had created itself without his thoughts. Most of the dragons only fly around the Glyderau Range, for they remain travelers of the night.

In one big sweep, the Trydan dragon knocks down thousands of Diablo Arches as they scream with agony, falling off their black horses and smashing to the ground in excruciating pain.

The head marquis commander of the Diablo Arches is Lylock. His oversized shoulders bulge from the sides of his chest plate. He waves one of his hands in the air to lead the rest of the Diablo Arches behind a huge rock to survive the deadly wing of the Trydan dragon. Lylock uses his magic power to summon their Rrysen dragons, which aren't part of a house but have the same size and functionality of a Trydan dragon.

One of the major differences between the two dragons is that the Rrysen has snake-like skin instead of the large scales of a Trydan. The Rrysen dragons give birth to thousands of four-legged Rhyfel beasts with sharp exoskeleton bodies. Most of the Rhyfel beasts detach themselves from under the wings of the huge Rrysen dragons. Most of them release quickly, thirsty for the fear of innocence of their prey, and the beasts fill the sky with their high-pitched voices. The Rhyfels have the ability to rip through metal with the tight grip of their poisonous fangs.

In unison, they climb over the land, approaching from all sides and surrounding Lancer and Ceri, who are already bracing for impact. Ceri raises her hand toward the arrows being shot by the Diablo Arches and extinguishes the flame from each red arrow as it falls dormant, snapping over the rocks nearby. One of the arrows misses Lancer's head by mere centimeters as he whips back from the arrowhead that slams into the rock and falls like the others.

Baron Milwr notices something is wrong with the Rhyfels; they are even attacking some of the Diablo Arches and killing some of the black horses as their squeals reach the skies. Lylock uses his large iron axe, which has the House of Diablo Arches coat of arms on the handle, to strike some of the Rhyfels' arrows that are coming his way. Yellow blood shoots from the exoskeletons of the Rhyfel beasts. Lylock begins freezing another Rhyfel that almost kills him as it pounces on him. Lylock smashes his fist through the head of a beast as it approaches from behind. On the other side, Ceri shoots down the Diablo Archwings from the sky as they crash onto the ground at massive speeds and explode. Other Rhyfels chomp their way through the high wind to get their prey or anything that moves toward their direction.

"We need to get out of here. Call for Drava immediately," Lancer says to Ceri. She raises her hand, shooting long waves of electricity throughout Glyder Fawr. A metallic sound pounds with energy. An earthquake shatters the ground, creating a huge crack below the Diablo Arches that are riding their black horses.

Most of them fall deep into the crack. The ground slams back together, sending thunderous vibrations across the land. Some of the Diablo Arches are crushed near the top of the crack, with arms, heads, and even horse body parts sticking out of the ground where the crack came back together.

Ceri's powers of electricity rip through most of the attackers. Lylock's son, Baron Milwr, whose voice is deadly when he speaks to anyone, begins to slowly speak to his father. Lylock wears a rare coronet with pink and canary-yellow diamonds, which are called Emosiwn Melyn. The diamonds have a special mineral that protects Lylock from being killed by his son's voice, which is a curse of Selwyn's Chancer for wars lost in the past. That's why every time Stratford comes around them, Stratford wears the same Emosiwn Melyn coronet around his long thick neck.

Baron and Lylock command all the wars of Selwyn's Chancer, since Stratford believed there was no need for them to waste his time fighting wars between trapped royal houses in Selwyn's Chancer. But this time the war backfired on them. Ceri's magical power is too strong for them when the moon is the brightest.

The last thing Lylock wants is the House of Cynfor moving ahead of them for the number two house in all the lands. The night becomes darker in twilight. Blood travels along the land around Glyder Fawr. Lancer and Ceri wonder how they are going to escape the situation when stars begin to sparkle on the horizon toward Y Garn. Commander Lylock yells out for the rest of his Archwings to head for the shadows of the mountains in the distance. Lancer and Ceri look on as the House of Diablo Arches flees. Baron Milwr leads them as his father, Lylock, rides into the shadow, disappearing in the nick of time as the sunrise appears over the Glyderau Range. The sun's rays bounce off their skin. Ceri picks up one of the dormant arrows from the ground then pulls her hood down further to block the sun from hitting her beautiful face. Signs of victory begin to fill their hearts as they look on.

"Until another day," says Lylock,

relaying his message from the clouds as their shadows disappear gracefully. Orange sunrays begin to flow over Glyder Fawr. A peregrine falcon flies above them with its shadow gliding slowly over the ground and Lancer's face.

Ceri, remaining unafraid, removes her crossbow, which was hidden inside her cloak. She looks left and notices blood dripping from Lancer's arm.

"You're hurt!" she screams. As she helps him take off his chest plate, Ceri notices a red arrow still twisting itself into Lancer's kidney. Once an arrow has penetrated his skin, the poisoned tip doesn't take full effect until an entire day has passed. After that, Lancer's body will begin to deteriorate until his flesh becomes harder than stone.

"I knew it hit me. You are lucky you didn't get hit," says Lancer as he pulls the arrow from his body and screams loudly. The tip of the arrow cuts his skin even more as it exits his wound. Lancer looks up, noticing the peregrine falcon looking at him from a rock directly across from them. The falcon starts using its beak to clean its feathers.

"Get away!" Ceri yells toward the bird. She screams out for her dragon, Drava, to swoop them up, and within a few minutes, a shadow glides above the clouds, sweeping down toward their location. Drava quickly lands, and its talons grip the dirt and rock. The peregrine falcon looks on as Ceri lifts Lancer, who is weak from the arrow wound. His face turns red as the poison moves throughout his bloodstream.

Drava roars loudly as it sweeps back into the sky, carrying Ceri and Lancer to Troia Nova. Ceri looks towards the ground below, the horses they where riding are butchered by the remaining Diablo Arches before sunrise.

As dawn breaks over the horizon, Ceri begins to think about Lancer and his health. She is silent as she sits on Drava's neck, traveling above the clouds to Troia Nova. Lancer is not dead but is in a deep sleep from exhaustion and dehydration from his injury. Lancer doesn't have much time to live. Ceri pulls her hood down further in disgrace, for Lancer and her father, Henry Gwynwell, who is now dead, remind her life is short. Drava starts adjusting its large wings due to some turbulence in the beautiful sky.

Ceri looks back and notices Verlock

and Alfred have magically appeared and are flying toward her. Ceri readjusts her hood and stays alert in case the twins begin to act up. Verlock and Alfred look at Lancer's bloody injury.

"We knew it would come to this," Alfred says with hesitation as Drava flies through an altocumulus lenticularis cloud formation. "We never wanted this to happen. Please understand, Ceri. You may notice Tim Hartwell should never have been allowed to find the Book of Hartwell. The power of the Galon will take its toll on his emotions sooner or later."

A few ice crystals form along the edges of their clothes due to the cirrus spissatus arrangements in the sky. Ceri, in fear of Lancer's health, taps on the neck of the dragon three times in a particular sequence of five taps, informing it to warm its body from the inside to heat its skin for them to stay warm. The skin of the dragon becomes transparent as Verlock looks down at the organs of the dragon moving inside its body. The dragon's skull looks massive and complex. Ceri looks over at the bones inside the wing structure, which has fire traveling through its veins.

"Would you look at that!" Verlock whispers loudly to Alfred.

"Pretty remarkable for her that she has the ability to warm her skin, for her mother could not," Ceri says, trying to keep herself calm. She pulls out another blanket to lay over Lancer's body.

"He doesn't have much time left,"

Alfred says, remaining callous, since he knows Tim Hartwell is their main concern.

"Thanks for reminding me," says Ceri. "Maybe you two should go back to where you came from. You aren't needed here anymore. We will be in Troia Nova shortly, so please leave us. I have a lot of deep thinking to do. My father is dead, my uncle is dying" Ceri adds.

"I don't want to seem rude. I just need some time alone with Lancer. Don't use your magic to get us there faster. That will do nothing but make Stratford know our location. If Lancer does pass away, he will pass without magic. He always told me to remember that, for that is the way he wants to die." Ceri looks up at the stars as day goes to night, the bright moon sliding from behind a cloud west of them. She looks back and sees a stratus cloud covering the royal blue sky.

Ceri turns around and notices Verlock and Alfred have disappeared into the night. She raises her right hand and looks at her father's signet ring. Using her left hand, she rubs the oval indentation on top of the ring and takes a deep breath. Without guidance, Ceri begins speaking to one of the stars in the sky. On this very night, a star from the Boötes constellation shines just enough to be seen with human eyes, which is thought to be a gift so people can contact someone dear to them. The message will be sent through the heavens.

"Father, oh Father. Will you look after Lancer? For I couldn't save him from death.

Father, can you hear me? I hope you are right about Tim Hartwell. He must be the one to free us all from Selwyn's Chancer. I hope you can hear my words of pain and agony. I will not fail again. I promise you dearly."

Ceri notices the star becoming brighter, for it listened to her every word. Ceri taps her Drava on the neck once more to speed up, get to Troia Nova, and have a proper funeral procession for her uncle, Lancer Gwynwell. She wipes her tears of sorrow as she and Lancer fly on the dragon through the clouds.

Ceri hopes for a better day ahead. To finally have her freedom is what she wants more than ever now. Ceri, with a serious expression on her face, is determined not to let anything ever get in her way again.

Funeral Games in Troia Nova

The sound of a commotion is coming from Brutus' palace. Early morning breaks above the horizon with a beautiful light-blue tone and an orange strip of color along the land. Some of the royal guards are in front of the temple of Diana, making sure no one enters. There is a large feast inside the palace. Brutus' top men and their lovely wives and children are sitting in their proper places to enjoy an early breakfast feast for Brutus and his unexpected guest, Tim Hartwell. The weather is cool but not too windy. Brutus and Tim sit in their places at the royal end of the table. Whispers about who Brutus brought sweep through the room. Everyone begins to eat. Children play with wooden swords outside the dinner hall, mimicking the great battles of leaders from their bedtime stories of Trojan ancestors.

Locrinus, Albanactus and Kamber arrive in the hall, taking their places next to their father, Brutus. Right away, Locrinus, the most outspoken, begins to speak to Tim about Tim's latest adventures.

"Welcome, Tim. Our father has told us much about your journey through Selwyn's Chancer. You are safe here. We have heard about your magical power. If you need anything from us, don't hesitate to ask." Locrinus makes Tim feel at home, while Kamber and Albanactus nod their heads in agreement. Tim begins to talk about a future location in the city of London.

"In my world, or what we call my present day or time, this very palace is where St. Paul's Cathedral rests. Brutus' stone, known as the London Stone, rests here and is dedicated to the arrival of Brutus on the Thames River."

Tim continues to talk about Great Britain becoming the United Kingdom with Queen Elizabeth II as heir. Brutus glances over, noticing his sons one by one taking in Tim's words, remembering every sentence he speaks. Brutus, in light of the situation, takes over the conversation.

"Tim, those words are food to our heart, but for now, let's talk about those moments in due time. We are all eager to hear the future of these lands and about my Trojan ancestors. But first, I haven't given you a formal introduction to my sons, Locrinus, Albanactus, and Kamber." Brutus points to each one of them as they begin to eat more of the delicious food on the table.

"Each one of my sons will take over these lands, for they have made me proud as a father." Brutus does not mention the mother of his children, for he feels it's not the right time to do so.

The entertainment arrives and catches everyone off guard. Musicians play their instruments and beautiful women dance, keeping the entire dining hall amused.

"Please, Tim. Come with me to the temple of Diana. I want to show you something I believe you would love to see." Brutus begins to unfold a few things for Tim to check out. Kamber picks up his glass, raising it for Tim in honor of his presence. Everyone at the table does the same as Brutus and Tim stand, return the toast, then proceed toward the arched exit. Brutus turns around for a quick second, raising his hand for Locrinus to take command of the feast while he is out. Locrinus nods; Brutus and Tim walk out of the palace and head to the temple.

The sun's rays glide between the columns of the temple, and the sky appears with an orange tone. Brutus and Tim walk through the pillars at the front of the temple. Brutus nods to his guards at the entrance. Tim hears the sound of a large fountain. His ears perk up as the wind comes inside the temple of Diana. A pool stretches from both ends of the temple, and a statue of Diana sits at the far end of the pool. Four torches burn, and a slight smell of incense comes from all four corners of the interior of the temple of Diana.

Brutus puts his hand on Tim's shoulder, guiding him over to the statue of Diana. Tim looks at it, amazed at the craftsmanship of the marble statue. Brutus asks the temple's interior guards to step outside with the rest of the guards so he can show Tim the reason he brought him to the temple. As the guards leave, Brutus looks at the stone wall then immediately pulls down a hidden lever in the wall.

A secret passage opens behind the statue of Diana. Brutus grabs one of the torches on the inside corner of the passage and heads down a stone stairwell. Making their way down the secret passage, Tim begins to adjust his messenger bag, wiping the sweat from his hands, not knowing what to expect. Brutus and Tim walk to the end of the passage, which opens to another marble pool area with three-meter-high ceilings. Tim notices a woman sitting at the other end of the pool. With disbelief, Tim knows in his heart that it must be someone very important. Brutus points toward the woman and tells Tim to walk over to her and introduce himself. Tim takes a long deep breath and slowly walks over while speaking to this mysterious tall woman with long brunette hair.

"My name is Tim, from the House of Hartwell." The woman turns to show her true identity as a beautiful goddess Diana.

"I know who you are, Tim. I am Diana, goddess of hunting. Welcome to my realm. I am very pleased to meet the boy all the gods are talking about. Your courage, honor, and sacrifice already mark you as a true man of respect from mighty Jupiter himself."

"How, are you here? I mean, why in the world are you in Selwyn's Chancer?" Tim looks over to Brutus who looks on as his right hand pulls his burgundy cape that's attached to his gold breast plate. Brutus adjusts the cloth around his wrist, thinks for a moment and unwraps the cloth, handing it to his new companion. Tim, with his mouth open, is shocked that such a legendary hero is giving him anything at all.

"We are here while you strive as a reflection in Selwyn's Chancer. You will only see what your destiny wants you to see. By the way, I noticed your training at Craig Cwm Silyn went well. Brutus did well, as the gods protected him like his ancestor, son of Prince Anchises and Goddess Venus, the son who traveled from Troy to the shores of Latium..."

Diana pauses for a moment as a small tear drips down her face into the water of the pool, flashing an image of Aeneas killing Turnus, then scenes of his escape from Troy. Some of the flashes show people in Latium, then King Latium crowning Aeneas the new ruler from a distant land. In a flash, the image disappears; the water goes back to normal with a halo of blue light moving through it. Diana, lost in the moment, uses her right hand to pull her hair behind her ears so it doesn't cover her face. She quickly gets back into her right frame of mind and continues to speak with a soft but strong voice that echoes throughout the room.

"You see, here you are, alive. Like Brutus, like Aeneas, your name will travel throughout the ages in your world and Selwyn's Chancer."

Tim looks toward Brutus who is looking on with eyes that believe every wise word

Diana speaks. Tim starts to think about his mother, Mary, back in Tenby, wondering about the consequences she faces because she gave him the Galon. Tim quickly focuses back on Diana.

"Stratford is getting stronger the more we speak, and things will change in this parallel world. It will eventually change your reality if you don't escape Selwyn's Chancer. Brutus, show Tim the London Stone, for he must break off a portion in two equal halves. Being the son, bearer of the Book of Hartwell and the Galon, will give you the power to succeed this obstacle. If you succeed, you will find the rope of Adamanthea with two more valuable gifts. It was handed down to me from the gods to give to Brutus as an award for reaching the shores of Troia Nova. Adamanthea's rope is one of the few things ever forged by the gods with enough magical power to get you back to your home alive.

"The power of the Galon will guide you in the depths of the Death of Ages to the Stairwell of Travel to get you back home. There is only one problem ahead of you, and that is Bledri and Tomes. You killed their father, Miniver and Cynhafar. Remember?"

Diana pulls her feet from the pool, drying them with a white cloth as she looks over to Brutus and Tim with a very serious look on her face.

"Brutus will guide you to the entrance of the Death of Ages to meet Darryn & Darron, the rulers of the House of Scorpus. They live on the reservoir of Llyn Cwellyn.

Brutus knows the way to find it. Don't forget that Darron is the smartest of the two rulers. He is the one you need to speak with about drinking the gwenwyna (Welsh: gwenwyn/ poison). It's made from an ancient box jellyfish. They squeeze poison extracted from the nematocysts on the jellyfish's tentacles. This poison will make you immune to the air you breathe while traveling the land in the Death of Ages.

Only the House of Cynfor, with its part dragon and part lionface creature, has the capability to survive there, unless you're a dead soul from Selwyn's Chancer. I must warn you that if the House of Cynfor even gets a smell of your existence down there, Bledri and Tomes will lock you in their dungeon forever. Your life, as we know it, will be punished by them for an eternity. There is a mid-aged barbarian who is gifted with his magical sword. Practicing wizardry has made him one of the most deadly people in all of Selwyn's Chancer. He goes by the name of Hynwyn Reese. He is the originator of the House of Scorpus, but after confrontations over power, Stratford damned him forever to the dungeons as a human being after Amelia married Stratford. Other prisoners who have been caught are good at stealing, so watch yourself down there, even around beasts from the underworld of Tartarus.

That being said, you won't be able to do it on your own. Young Ceri will be your help, Tim Hartwell."

Diana looks over to one of the fires

torches burning on the wall. Tim wonders why she didn't mention Lancer. "Besides," Diana says, "I would love to send Brutus there to help you. Unfortunately, he has to fulfill his destiny along with his three sons back in his time."

"Aren't we in Selwyn's Chancer?" asks Tim. "Didn't Lancer found these lands? You know, the city of London already existed, Diana." Tim speaks with the magical power of the Galon that incites a rage within him. His emotions continue to grow with an unpredictable outcome.

"One day you will understand," Diana slowly replies as she walks back over to Tim. Brutus tosses the cloth that's around his wrist to Diana. She ties it around Tim's wrist and says, "Brutus must honor you, for this scarf you are wearing was made by Hector's wife, Andromache, long before Brutus was even born. Hector asked her to make it, for he had a dream in which he was informed by the gods that Brutus of Troy, the grandson of his third cousin, including principle lieutenant Aeneas, would also be legends themselves discovering new foreign lands. So Andromache made the cloth, giving it to Hector to hand to the gods. Brutus wore it, and now is the time for you to have it, Tim, for you will need it more than ever."

Diana nods to Brutus with the utmost honor and respect for giving away something so priceless to the Trojan bloodline, just as the sword of Troy was given to Aeneas by Prince Paris. Diana touches part of the Trojan symbol on the cloth wrapped around

Tim's wrist. Brutus is quiet, knowing he loves to help others. He nods back and sticks out his chest with honor.

"Even though the end of your destiny is unclear, be safe. Remember love, honor, and to keep loyalty in your soul to heal the world," says Diana, winding down her speech. "You will leave on the sunrise of the thirteenth day. Brutus, your son, Albanactus, is riding here to the temple to let you know about your friends arriving from their long flight escaping the attack of Lylock and his treacherous son Baron Milwr."

"You mean Ceri and Lancer?" Tim blurts out with anticipation.

"Yes, now go," Diana quickly replies.

Brutus and Tim dash upstairs to the main gallery of the temple. Albanactus is already standing by the entranceway to the temple and begins to call out Brutus' name, just like Diana predicted. Brutus pulls the lever back up to the secret passage, shutting the door behind him. They rush over to the entranceway where Albanactus is standing with the guards from outside. The two interior guards are quickly ordered by Brutus to head back into the temple and keep watch. Tim looks at some of the guards from the temple as Albanactus stands there with his armor and royal cape as well. He is always ready for war.

"Father, your guests have arrived," says Albanactus. One of them is badly wounded. Procter believes he's dead."

"Thank you, my son. Let's get over there and see exactly what's going on.

Tell your brothers to meet us at the inner courtyard to the palace."

Brutus gives a few more orders to other soldiers to watch the area around Troia Nova with the rest of the ground soldiers. Albanactus has brought two extra horses for Brutus and Tim to get back to the palace. Albanactus rides back faster than lightning, with electricity coming from the horse's feet. Brutus and Tim ride along with the sun high in the sky, and a short, cool breeze blows. As they ride, Tim wonders about his mother, Mary. Her love for him, he believes, is unmatched. Tim has flashes in his head of Tenby, Pembrokeshire, during the winter as the snow falls onto the water. He remembers drinking tea and eating his favorite Welsh bacon and laver bread.

Tim understands that love, honor, and loyalty mean more to him now than being captive in the world of Selwyn's Chancer.

Everyone arrives back at Brutus' palace. They look up at Ceri's dragon standing in the middle of the inner courtyard of Brutus palace. Walking through the entrance of the inner courtyard, Tim sees Procter, the palace's doctor, using moist cloths to soak up the blood from Lancer's body. The cloths are dipped with special ingredients called ambrosia and nectar. Inner guards of the palace make their way into the courtyard. Tim runs over to Ceri, bumping a few people along the way. He notices Lancer in the arms of Ceri, who remains cold inside. Brutus' three sons run to their father, looking toward the silent courtyard. Kamber raises his eyes, staring at Ceri's dragon. Ceri remains quiet.

"Ceri, what happened? How did Lancer die?" Tim asks slowly.

Ceri stops swaying for a moment. "We were ambushed at Lyn Lydaw. Glyder Fawr, to be exact. The House of Diablo Arches was ready for us. I'm thinking Stratford knew about our plans to get more help. If Stratford wanted you both dead you would be. He is keeping you alive, Tim. He knows you are trapped in Selwyn's Chancer. Lancer sacrificed his life, like my father, for Tim to set us free." Ceri wipes some dirt from Lancer's cold face. Brutus looks on, feeling the warmth of Ceri's words as he gives orders for procedures that have taken place since the beginning of Troy.

"First, we must give him a proper burial. We will have funeral games for twelve days in honor of Lancer." Brutus points his finger at his royal servants to attend to Lancer's body and prepare the pyre with extra wood from the royal cellar. Brutus tells Locrinus to lead Ceri to her quarters so she can dress in the proper clothing.

Albanactus shows Tim to his quarters so he can get ready, which leaves Brutus in the inner courtyard with the dragon. He looks into Drava's large bright eyes.

"Hello, my friend. Ceri's magical power must be strong for you to be tamed."

Drava takes one step away from Brutus, unafraid but not wanting to be touched by anyone except Ceri and a few others by misjudgment.

Chapter 3: Funeral Games in Troia Nova?

"Are you telling me Kamber can pet you and I can't?" Brutus adds some humor, "Well, the ladies have always liked Kamber." He smiles. "Now I see why." Brutus laughs for a moment as the Drava leaps high into the air, thrusting its body into the clouds and twirling three hundred and sixty degrees. "Pretty impressive," Brutus whispers to himself, walking back to the entranceway of the palace and to his king's chamber to get ready for tonight's remembrance.

Ceri and Locrinus walk down the royal hall to Ceri's guest quarters. Locrinus wishes her well before he dashes off to get ready himself. Ceri walks through her doorway, which is made from some of the best wood in the land. A golden door handle reflects her movements as she notices a long white cloak with a hood, which is another special request from Brutus. Ceri walks over to a mirror sparkling on the wall near the closet. She sits next to the cloak, breathing for a second, then hops into the hot premade bath in the marble tub. Some of Lancer's blood, which had dried on her arms, begins to swirl in the water. Ceri pulls her hair back then raises her hand, looking at Henry Gwynwell's signet ring again. Flashes of her father and Lancer's death race through her head. Ceri begins to cry, her tears dropping into the bath water. The flashes stop when a male voice across the room sounds familiar to her ears.

"Father!" Ceri screams in panic. "Father, Lancer is dead. Mark my words Father, that after tonight, you will have to watch over him." Suddenly, her father Henry begins to speak, but not as a ghost. He's something more than that.

"I will protect him, Ceri. Your words mean so much, my daughter. Tim will be able to help you in Selwyn's Chancer. Listen to him. But remember, you are now the last living House of Gwynwell descendant." Henry pauses for a moment, then picks up where he left off. "Make us proud. Stay strong and remember not to look back to old memories. Live for the now; live for yourself. Live for the House of Gwynwell."

Henry's words fade into thin air as Ceri screams, wanting her father to stay with her. Two female servants run into the room, thinking Ceri is being attacked. Ceri snaps out of her trance and quickly shouts, "Do not enter this room!" Ceri demands them to stay in the bedroom area.

The elder servant, not wasting any time, says from the bedroom, "A thousand apologies, my lady. Are you all right? We thought you were in trouble." The younger servant breathes hard from running down the royal hall.

"My lady Ceri," says the elder servant, "It's time for you to get dressed. The pyre has been constructed, and Lancer's body has been covered in the finest silk. Bundles of roses have been spread across the inner section of the courtyard. Locrinus crafted a special torch, which he calls a priceless gift from the gods."

Ceri orders the servants to turn around so they can't see her face as she walks into the bedroom, drying her hair with a towel. As Ceri changes into her white cloak, the younger servant looks into the mirror, trying to get a better look at Ceri's face. Using a bit of magic, Ceri points her index finger toward another folded robe on a seat that lifts up and covers the servants face who is trying to look at her.

"You know, it's rude to stare!" Ceri says to the young servant.

"Don't mind her, my lady. She is young and foolish and has never seen a Gwynwell descendant before."

The older servant says to the younger, "Now apologize to Ceri for being rude."

"With my deepest apologies, my lady. I mean you no disrespect. I admire your hair, for I wish I had beautiful hair like yours," says the younger servant while rubbing her short hair with her hands.

"I accept your apology," Ceri replies, then cuts a small lock of hair from her head and adds a green ribbon around one end to keep it together. Ceri raises the hood on the white cloak, pulling it down, covering her face as she walks over to the younger servant and places the hair in her hand. The servant cries with passion, feeling honored to know Ceri Gwynwell.

Ceri and the servants walk out of the guest chamber into the royal hallway. Both sides of the hall have guards, workers, and lower-level servants standing shoulder to shoulder. Candles glow in their hands, and some members of the royal choir begin to sing the Hymns of Torment. Ceri looks right as the main hall servant hands her the unlit torch as she walks under the open archway leading into the courtyard. Hymns fill the hallway all the way to the courtyard where more melodies are released in unison. Ceri, a bit nervous, places the torch in her opposite hand and wipes the sweat from her now-empty palm. Voices of joy and sorrow fill the sky. Ceri looks toward Tim standing next to Brutus and his three sons, their wives, and the personal counsel all dressed in white linen robes. Everyone is sitting to the left of the pyre, holding the hands and arms of their loved ones.

Hymns continue to fill the air. The sky is dark blue, reflecting onto the onlookers' skin as their white robes glow slightly from the magic shine of the moon. Everyone is awaiting Ceri's arrival. Torches are lit on a stake with rectangle edges. Orange-colored fires burn at medium height so as not to overpower the shadows. Ceri's torch is still unlit as the hymns reach maximum capacity. She walks to the side of the wooden stairwell leading to the top of the pyre. Tim knows his time has come to honor the death of a new friend. He stands with his chest sticking out and walks over to Ceri to give her some encouragement with a minor hug and two kisses on each cheek.

Tim places two coins in her hand then looks up and yells "Firewyn," igniting the blue-colored flame. Tim raises his illuminated hand over the torch with a blessing of peace. The flame turns back to its normal light-orange flame. Tim nods his head for

Ceri to make her way to the top of the pyre. She walks up the stairs in a way that could seem to be slow motion. Everyone looks up at her as she screams "Father!" Her voice reaches higher than the moving clouds.

Ceri glances down placing two coins over Lancer's eyes. She looks at the pale skin on his face and body. She then looks up at the stars and puts the head of the torch inside the stack of wood that surrounds Lancer's body from underneath. The fire burns high in the sky, the wood begins to crackle, and pieces of ash with flaming tips glide into the air.

Ceri looks on with her heart in the right place. This sign of peace soothes her mind, and she finally feels all right about his safe passage with Charun to the underworld.

The fire reflects onto Ceri's eyes, and the fire reaches high into the sky. Everyone looks at Ceri, standing with her legs in a wider stance. Brutus looks over to his sons, knowing he would never want to see himself burying them. He looks at some of his council, then places his hand over his heart. The entire crowd in the courtyard is silent.

Tim begins to have a weird feeling inside. He pulls his white cloak further up one of his arms and looks toward a particular star in the Boötes constellation. Everything around Tim freezes as a star brighter than the others, which is the vision for the 5th Galon, begins to whisper in his ear. Many unknown voices tell him about the beginning of magic and the original creation of human beings, along with Selwyn's Chancer.

The coordinates over the heart of the herdsman read:

RA14h41m24.24s D37°57'25.64'

The letters, numbers and symbols illuminate the sky over the constellation in Boötes. Everyone around Tim, including Lancer's pyre, is frozen from the power of the Galon. Tim unfreezes. Everyone, including Brutus, has no clue about what just happened. Only Tim was able to see and hear the star from Boötes. Brutus' wife, Ignoge, who loves to stay out of the picture most of the time, holds her husband's hand. Her eyes shine as hymns are sung long into the night. Royal servants bring food to eat as they continue to watch the pyre burn.

Everyone's heart is open with the utmost respect for Ceri's lost ones. Her mind is curious, even about the funeral games.

Many hours later the melodies fade out along with the fire on the pyre. Throughout the night, the entire small city of Troia Nova sleeps. The pyre has gone out in the inner courtyard. A little smoke exits the bottom part of the pyre. Silence has swept throughout the palace except for the sounds of nature. Some of the royal guards are walking their shifts to make sure everything's in order around the palace.

Dawn breaks and the sun begins to lift over the horizon displaying dark-orange, medium-dark royal blue, and grey hues. Brutus wakes up early, knocking on Tim's door a few hours before the funeral games begin.

"Wake up, Tim." Brutus shows him

some courtesy before he walks in to wake him up. Tim rubs his eyes and gets out of bed, throwing on some of the new clothes Brutus gave him to wear. Tim throws his messenger bag carrying the Book of Hartwell inside a locking cabinet and heads over to the door with Brutus. Walking down a few hallways and around a few corners, Tim follows Brutus as he heads left toward his royal vault inside the his palace.

As they reach the entranceway to the vault, Tim notices nine guards with enormous shields and armor guarding the door as if their lives depend on it. Brutus salutes his royal guards as they stand down. The guards walk to the opposite sides of the vault door and lift a defensive, rectangular slab of stone from metal latches on the enormous vault door. Another guard walks in front of the left side of the large door while the other moves to the right. Both of them push the door, which splits in two as they slowly open it. Brutus and Tim walk over to the entrance, and Tim notices treasure from wall to wall.

"These are some of the most special treasures I have collected inside my own world," says Brutus. "Some of them have been through many ages. There are also treasures from Troy that Agamemnon has never seen. My grandfather was able to get them out of the city in time. You see, much of the future we already knew. Diana told me to move across the lands." Brutus smiles, taking a few treasures as they walk over to another room inside the vault with armor, weapons, luxurious cloths, glasses, and diamonds covering extended tables that are neatly stacked.

Brutus walks over to dark royal-blue drapes with the picture of Adamanthea on them. Brutus uses his right hand to pull the drapes aside to let Tim walk in. Tim immediately looks at a simple light coming from the ceiling inside this separate marble room. There is a stone circle surrounding a milestone in the middle of the room. Brutus points to one of the stones on the floor.

"This stone in your generation will be known as the London Stone, for the smaller grey-colored stone you have already touched in Totnes. I had it placed there, cracking it away from the part of the ground when I first arrived on the banks of my New

Troy," Brutus says. "Diana has blessed me to get here. That is why I thank the gods every day for helping me achieve my destiny. The secrets from the gods will now be laid upon you. My grandfather's father, Anchises, bred horses, which were given to him by Laomedon from Zeus. Not too many mortals know these stories."

Brutus unsheathes his sword, striking the milestone with all of his might. He uses his strength and power to knock a corner slab as big as a watermelon off the London Stone. Brutus points to the stone with his sword. Tim remembers what Diana said about cracking this large stone in two equal halves.

Tim, getting some inner strength, opens his heart of courage and uses the magical power of the 5th Galon. He raises his fist and smashes his hand on top of the London Stone.

"CRACK"

"The power of the Galon proves to be very trustworthy for you, Tim," says Brutus, pleased with the outcome as Tim stands next to the cracked stone below his feet. "The gods favor you. Cherish this moment."

Brutus shows Tim something sticking out of the cracked milestone. Brutus reaches down, picking up Adamanthea's rope along with two pieces of rubble that broke away from the same stone.

"These two small pebbles will turn into those horses given to Laomedon for Anchises. They never age or die, like Adamanthea herself. These horses, made by Zeus, are designed to never tire, never thirst, and to walk through fire hotter than the sun." Brutus notices Tim looking down, rubbing the rope grain. "When you reach the Death of Ages, plant the pebbles in the soil and watch them grow from the earth like trees in a forest." Brutus points to some of the horse paintings engraved on the walls that show a sequence of how the horses grow from the ground.

"You and Ceri will use these horses to ride the lands of the Death of Ages. Diana knows you need these things to survive, for I learned from her about the bigger challenges in life. Understanding the obstacles in life will always be the wise man's strength. Hear me speak, as the kings before me told me to trust my heart and nothing will be able to stop me from reaching my destiny. I have heard of your great power from Lancer himself. I am now a believer of your magical ability after you cracked the unbreakable milestone with ease."

Mighty Brutus hands Adamanthea's brownish-red rope to Tim, who holds it in front of him and puts the two small pebbles in his pocket.

"What exactly does this do?" asks Tim, looking at the beautiful handcrafted rope.

"Adamanthea's rope will make your body hover between the sky, sea, and Mother Earth, Mr. Hartwell. That is the only way to escape Selwyn's Chancer, guard it with your life."

Brutus hands Tim Adamanthea's rope, which starts to illuminate like a green aurora in the sky. The handle of the rope has a ruby cap at the bottom. Tim looks more confident than ever now that he knows magic of this magnitude. Not too long ago he was just a small, unpopular kid from Tenby, Pembrokeshire.

"The power of the Galon, along with the presence of the Book of Hartwell and Adamanthea's rope," Tim whispers to himself as his heart begins to open at the possibility of saving everyone from Stratford's Selwyn's Chancer spell. Suddenly, Tim looks around and notices he is not in Troia Nova anymore.

Tim and Brutus are suspended between the earth, sky and sea by the power of Adamanthea's rope. They look up and see space leading toward the Boötes constellation. Tim and Brutus can see the voices of many different artificial intelligence species from planets light years away. The planets begin moving in a wide circular motion. Tim notices that the Boötes constellation is shining its light in a weird offset sequence.

"Is time really on my side?" Tim asks the star as Brutus looks over at him.

"Only time will tell," the mysterious voice replies with a deep tone.

"Using Adamanthea's rope, you may enter the sublevels of Selwyn's Chancer on your planet. Some of them have forests filled with beautiful lands, which all mimic the older times of Snowdon."

The unknown voice is cut off by Amelia and Stratford, who magically appear suspended next to Brutus and Tim.

Stratford has watched enough and needs to speak his mind.

Stratford is dressed in black clothes, and a silver breastplate covers his chest. He looks over at Brutus, knowing Brutus is ready for war at any moment. Stratford moves his hand over the sword that's attached to the side of his belt. The twin Wyvern gargoyles, Verlock and Alfred, appear next to them under Stratford's control. Their eyes flame red and their faces have a dark-grey tone. Alfred snaps his fingers, magically sending everyone into the Guildhall in present time. It is night and they are sitting at a large circular dinner table. Stratford has made Verlock and Alfred his personal slaves.

"Well, well, well, if it isn't the legendary Brutus of Troy," Stratford says as he eats some of the roasted pork on his plate. A few slaves, dressed in clothes from the 1800s, continue to bring exotic-looking food. "The slaves were given to me by the House of Diablo Arches. They are helpful, aren't they?" Stratford says to Amelia before turning to Tim and Brutus who are sitting across the table.

"This gathering will be short. Tim, if you really think I'm going to let you out of Selwyn's Chancer with the Book of Hartwell, you are wrong, dear boy. You may keep the power of the Galon. Doesn't that sound like a good deal?" says Stratford, using his sneaky tactics.

"Brutus, I am amazed to see you here. Such family history to be in my world. Such an honor." Stratford smirks while Amelia puts her arm around him, giving him a quick kiss for more confidence. "You won't last forever. I am here to make sure Tim will fulfill his very own destiny."

Brutus throws a few words over to Stratford to get a rise out of him. "Nice one, Brutus. I am no longer worried about you, for your destiny, even in my world, won't permit me to change those events in time."

Stratford looks directly at Brutus, knowing the facts. He turns his head toward Tim, as his neck turns almost like that of a cobra snake.

"Tim Hartwell, aren't you supposed to be having funeral games for Ceri?" says Amelia, wanting to pick a fight. "Doesn't she need you right now? How could you leave her alone?"

Stratford looks at Amelia to let her know he will take over the conversation. "Oh, Lancer. How much I have forgotten. The only reason he is dead is because members of the House of Gwynwell put their nose in business that didn't concern them. I am not the most evil person at heart, so you will tell Ceri she will have her twelve days of funeral games for Lancer," says Stratford, somehow showing a bit of compassion for a lost one.

"Remember, Tim, I have control of Verlock and Alfred now. They will tell me everything you do from now on. Since you have collected all seven Galons, they won't be able to help you like they did before. They already told me your mother, Mary, had the 1st Galon and that she helped you along the way. I hope she knows what she got herself into, for I don't think you could possibly understand."

Amelia hears a noise coming from inside the room. Stratford orders two beasts with trousers and linen shirts to walk into the Great Hall and pass the stone walls behind him for protection.

The chandeliers refract light near their table. Stratford looks up near the red drapes, which begin to move on the balcony above them. A dragon with the head of a dragon and the head of a lion jumps over the balcony to the lower level where everyone is sitting.

"Bledri and Tomes?" Alfred whispers to his beloved twin.

"I could kill that boy right now!" Bledri

says with a mean tone.

"You don't even want a piece of him, dragon boys. Tim could put you both in your father's shoes, dead," Amelia says, poking fun at the new rulers of the House of Cynfor. She uses her magic to slide another long table between them and everyone else.

Bledri and Tomes are wearing steel-forged metal. Leather straps hold their chest plate. Amelia uses her magic and turns them into humans with royal clothing, including blazers with the House of Cynfor coat of arms on the shoulder.

"This should be the way you look when you're invited to dinner," says Amelia, smiling at Tim to show that she and Stratford have them completely under control. Stratford raises his hand and rubs Amelia's chin, for what she does for him goes unmatched.

"Tim, you will continue to have your twelve days of funeral games," Stratford says gracefully.

Bledri is jealous because they weren't given a special time to mourn their father. Bledri pleads to Stratford to let them bring Tim to Selwyn's Chancer and kill him.

"No! You will have your time soon enough, Bledri and Tomes." Stratford claps his hands, sending Tim and Brutus back into Troia Nova's palace so he can have a private conversation with Bledri and Tomes.

Stratford scolds them for being so hardheaded. "Do you really think I am going to let them live in peace?" Stratford points in their direction with a grin on his face. "Remember, I give the orders around here. This is my world, and I will do whatever I see fit to keep order." Stratford forces his words out, trying to prove a point. Bledri, not feeling Stratford's aggression, says what's exactly on his twisted mind.

"What about your verbal agreement with the House of Diablo Arches making them the number two house in all of Selwyn's Chancer?" Slime oozes from between Blendri's teeth and out his mouth, accentuating his nasty dragon breath. Stratford ignores what Bledri says, except for his last two points.

"First off, you imbeciles, I name who is in charge. Yes, they are the number two in all of the houses, but I can say the House of Diablo Arches has completely destroyed keeping order within Selwyn's Chancer.

Lylock can be foolish, but his son has the voice to kill anyone, which I need right now so you can keep the Emosiwn Melyn diamonds flowing in the Death of Ages," Stratford says, as he reasons with Bledri and Tomes on the power of rule over the *Caves of Siôr* diamond caves.

The rulers of the House of Cynfor smile but are still unhappy about the house arrangements. Stratford gives them a chance to have something a little more meaningful.

"In the meantime, I will send Tim's mother, Mary, to your collection of prisoners in your vicious dungeon. Keep her in the large tower of your castle. I will send many legions of Rhyfels to attack Tim and Brutus' entourage during Lancer's funeral games.

I will summon Baron Milwr and Lylock to fly their Rrysen dragons over their location to drop off legions of their four-legged, slimy, and disgusting eight-eyed spiders. Let's play with Tim and Brutus' entourage. I will give Tim and Brutus good reason to come down to the Death of Ages, and you will lead them into a trap so Tim is stuck there forever and ever!"

Stratford laughs out loud and continues his rant in an evil voice. "Mary is the key to trapping Tim, Bledri. Have you forgotten that Tim easily killed your father, Miniver, and Cynhafar? He could do the same to you both. You will have your day to avenge your father's death. Bledri, you and Tomes head back down to your castle and I will inform you when you need to get your house ready for the transformation ritual.

Out of nowhere, Tomes, the other head on Bledri's dragon body, says, "Yes, my lord master."

"Oh, my. A lionface that speaks? I see your house has been keeping up with other languages, Bledri," Stratford says, knowing it is rare for the lionface to speak. "By the way, what have you done with Hynwyn Reese? Please tell me."

Bledri begins to laugh and says, "We have him working in the Caves of Siôr. We've also been using him for his sword ability in the Carantoc gladiator games. He has made us very wealthy, I might add."

"I see," says Stratford. "Do what you must. This gives me less of a headache about the overcapacity in the dungeons.

You must control the killings down there. If I hear Reese has been killed due to your petty games, I will destroy you both. Do you read me loud and clear?"

Stratford demands them to answer. Bledri and Tomes both nod as Amelia makes them disappear back to the Death of Ages.

Amelia holds her wine glass and sits next to Stratford. They both look toward the stage. The lights dim inside the Great Hall when an orchestra begins to play. Drums pound along to a catchy melody. The burgundy curtains open to nine ballet dancers, all in their positions, who move gracefully across the stage when the strings strike. Amelia looks at Stratford, kissing him. "All this for me?" Amelia asks excitedly, for she knows what he does not: a male child of Stratford's grows in her womb as she rubs her stomach.

Brutus wraps his arm around her neck, watching the white hawk of battle performance. "Is that Gavina? I hear she is the best dancer in all of Selwyn's Chancer, except for you, my love," he says. "Would you do me the honor and dance with me?" Stratford treats Amelia with a lot more respect, knowing that without her witchcraft, he would be useless ruling Selwyn's Chancer, even if he created it.

Both of them begin dancing along the burgundy carpet while the ballet dancers on the stage, unfazed, continue their act. Stratford lets go for a moment as he dances the night away with Amelia in the Guildhall.

Back in Troia Nova, Tim and Brutus find

themselves in the same royal vault as if they had never left. They walk out and head for the garden area to get the funeral games organized. Brutus tells his event organizers to have archery competitions with some of the most dangerous and fastest animals in all of Selwyn's Chancer. He then informs them to add the chariot race, along with a chasing match by the last living giant titan, Magog, the son of Gogmagog who has was found hiding in Merlin's cave.

Procter begins to speak to Brutus with some humor. "Being trampled by giants always gets your heart pumping, especially Corineus' victory over Gogmagog, my king." Procter hopes he doesn't have to do that competition, for he has never been a soldier of battle. He is fine with being the royal doctor for Brutus and his family; he is not the adventurous type.

Locrinus walks in from the right, wanting to hear more about the games. "Father, will we be ready to leave soon?"

"Yes, my son. Get your arrows ready, for I am ready to watch the games. I hear Ceri is pretty good herself. Where is she, by the way?" Brutus asks his son.

"She's still in the courtyard of the pyre," Locrinus says, looking over his shoulder wondering where Ceri is as well.

"Let's round everyone up and head over to the south bank of the Thames River. We will start there," says Brutus to everyone around him.

"We call it Battersea Park in my time," Tim says with a confident tone.

"Is that so?" Locrinus answers very curiously. "I would be pleased to hear more about the future of these lands." Locrinus is intrigued about the future in general.

"You will soon enough, my son, for those parts of the land will be yours to rule someday," says Brutus, pointing out some of his son's future.

Ceri walks out with her hood up, looking reserved but ready to start the games in honor of Lancer. Everyone begins departing for the south bank. On their way there, a royal guard rides up to his ruler and commander from Troia Nova and says, "My king, word comes from our world at home. The Ark of the Covenant was stolen by the Philistines who are en route back to the Philistine Pentapolis."

Brutus curls his lip. "I heard of the Battle of Aphek, so the story of the Ark and the words spoken by God are true." Brutus rubs his chin as he rides his horse, ending his speech as the messenger runs back into position toward the south part of Troia Nova.

Startled, Tim says, "How can you know such things while in Selwyn's Chancer?"

"Remember, Tim, I was brought here only to train you at Mynydd Graig Goch. After the funeral games, I am going to take you to the gates of the Death of Ages to get you on your journey home. Ceri's father, Henry Gwynwell, and Lancer are the reason I was even able to be here in front of you. Well, maybe a little of Diana's help too," Brutus laughs, giving more words of encouragement to the young and gifted wizard as they make their way down the cold river Styx.

The sky is blue and rich, and God's rays cover the land. Wild horses run along the ground not too far off. Tim's intuition begins to grow stronger, for he can smell vibes of war in the air. He knew Stratford was acting suspiciously. At this moment, nothing seems to add up about Stratford not trying to steal the Book of Hartwell. Tim knows something is up. For this, he is ready.

Battle on the River Thames

All of the horses break out of a forest near the river. The royal workers have set up the funeral games' archery event. The sun is bright and shining during a beautiful afternoon with birds flying in the air. Kamber, out of the corner of his eye, notices a falcon flying above them. Ceri remembers that this is the same peregrine falcon she saw when she was with Lancer back in Glyder Fawr.

"Tim, I've seen that falcon before!" Ceri yells, giving warning to her comrades.

She looks over at Tim while everyone who was riding with them is at the other end of the archery range.

Albanactus, ready to show his ability, shouts at the top of his lungs, "I will murder this creature. Observe." Albanactus quickly pulls an arrow with white feathers from its carrying case on his back, shooting it faster than thunder. Tim looks on as the main crowd turns from the range. Brutus shields his eyes with his hand to get a better look at the mark above in the sky.

Ceri notices Kamber and Locrinus looking at a cumulonimbus cloud approaching not too far off from the falcon's location in the air. The arrow hits the peregrine as a river of black feathers sprays over the land as far as they can see. The sky turns from day to night in a flash. The entire camp looks on with disbelief. Locrinus and Brutus, almost speaking in unison, scream their orders to the royal soldiers. Locrinus sends a few soldiers back to the palace to send word to all of the people in Troia Nova to stand guard, for the magic of Selwyn's Chancer has made its move.

Brutus, along with his sons and royal soldiers, gets into formation for the attack. Locrinus and Albanactus unsheathe their razor sharp swords.

Kamber notices the size of a massive Trydan dragon coming out of another cumulonimbus cloud. A dark night turns into complete blackness.

"This is not good at all," Tim says. Illuminations from small explosions brighten the troposphere up to the stratosphere. The Trydan dragon flies with a different unknown energy along its tail. Small explosions go off randomly underneath the Trydan's wings. Ceri, looking up unfazed, has seen this same action before.

Millions of high-pitched screams and explosions flood the skies. The Rhyfel spiders have detached themselves and are flying down toward Tim and the rest of the group like bombs out of a jet. Rhyfel screams grow louder and louder until Brutus commands his royal archers to start shooting their fire-tipped arrows into the sky. Ceri uses her magic power to blow the arrows like bombs to brighten the lands as they explode in the sky with deep snapping tones. Some of the arrows explode packs of Rhyfel bodies;

some blow half of their eyes out of their ugly eight-eyed faces.

"Die!!!" Ceri yells with a crazy, vengeful tone. She uses her magic power to shoot green electrical currents into the sky, blasting through thousands of Rhyfels. Tim is ready to end this attack and loudly screams **"FIREWYN!"**

Brutus turns to see what Tim is about to do. Kamber, being aggressive, also kills many spiders with his arrows. Tim, using the power of the 1st and 5th Galon, ignites the blue flame in his hands. A blinding light whips through the sky, freezing every Rhyfel spider in the air. The spider bodies above them are four meters high with nasty, hairy legs and glaring spider eyes. Some of their bodies are positioned in weird ways: legs up, legs down, sideways. Some are even separated from their body parts that were hit in the sky as hemolymph, or blood, begins to ooze out of some of their bodies. Tim wonders why the hemolymph is moving but their bodies aren't.

"Now that's what I call a magic trick," Kamber says, taking a deep breath.

"Their legs are really long. Do you see those things?" Albanactus adds.

Brutus orders everyone to light their torches. The sky begins to illuminate with its darker red color at the horizon. They begin to make their way back to the palace. Ceri and everyone else feels hurt that she wasn't able to honor Lancer's death. Stratford's lies have gotten the best of her.

Brutus tells everyone to remain close

as the moon sneaks from behind one of the clouds above them. A cemetery of millions of Rhyfel spiders frozen in the sky almost creates a canopy, and there are jagged shadows on the ground. Ceri looks up past the roof of dead Rhyfel bodies and notices the Trydan dragon flying back into one of the huge greyish clouds.

"Well, aren't you smart," Tim whispers to himself as Ceri begins to unfold the history of the Trydan dragons being one of the oldest royal houses in all of magical Selwyn's Chancer.

"The House of Diablo Arches shouldn't be ignored either," says Ceri, "for only Lylock and Baron Milwr have the magic to hatch Rhyfel spiders that live in cocoons underneath the Trydan's wings.

Unfortunately, Stratford's world is changing every day around us. Once you stepped one foot here, Tim, the world began to change. Even Henry noticed it. Believe me, he was always telling me about a male descendant from the House of Hartwell who would eventually free our people from the unbearable prison of Stratford's spell.

"Fear is only an illusion. Dream big, Tim. I was born to think that way, and you should think that way too. No matter what you believe, remember to fulfill your destiny."

Brutus starts to walk the moist grounds, checking his people as the air begins to get colder by the second.

With luck, the dead bodies above them gradually clear up with only a few Rhyfel spiders suspended in the air.

Thirty royal guards and event organizers are making their way out of the path of the dead spiders. Somehow, millions of spider bodies made from Emosiwn Melyn diamonds suddenly appear. Their long legs cut through the people trapped beneath them. The survivors look on with horror.

CLASHHH!

The Rhyfel bodies smash the remaining royal guards and their horses to the ground, sounding like a million wine bottles dropping onto concrete. Brutus looks at some of his people dying terrible deaths filled with pain and agony. Their screams are muffled by the blood that leaves their poor souls drifting away in the night.

The Rhyfel spider bodies are sharper than glass and break into a million pieces over the lands. The spiders were designed by the House of Diablo Arches from blueprints that came from breaking down all of the secret elements that make up Emosiwn Melyn diamonds.

Tim, Brutus, Albanactus, Kamber, and Locrinus stand there, dumbstruck at the sight of death from dishonor by Stratford, who leaves his soldiers without a proper burial. Brutus raises his hand as Tim watches Albanactus throw his father a golden box with a rope dangling from its corner. Brutus places his hand over the box, and the rope lifts without the box opening. A mist of remembrance made from a nectar oil blessed by the gods begins to flow from the box, moving toward all of the bodies that were trapped underneath the Rhyfel's when they fell. Brutus puts his hands together, and everyone follows him. One of the royal soldiers with the royal family tosses a torch where the bodies lie helpless without life flowing through their veins.

Everyone steps back, looking at the fire rising high into the air as it turns yellow from an orange-red color. It reflects in their eyes as they watch their comrades burn away up in sky.

The emotions in the camp are subdued. Tim can't even utter a whisper or phrase. Brutus, sitting tall on his horse, swings one of his arms around, giving the order to ride back to the royal palace. The pack bursts into the forest from whence it came heading back to Troia Nova.

"No funeral games for Lancer?"

Ceri whispers in her mind while feelings run deep in the camp members' veins. Most of them want revenge to honor their loved ones. Their hearts are not filled with hatred, however, for most of them understand that when a person dies, one must be happy no matter what because they are going to a better place. Not one soul questions the gods at Troia Nova. All that is within them is the Trojan blood that holds the agony from one of the greatest wars of all mankind, the fall of Troy.

The sun breaks over the horizon right around the time the group makes it back to Troia Nova. Every family member of the soldiers comes running out. Wives kiss their husbands as they hold their loved ones who have made it back alive.

"The Diablo Arches will be back," Ceri says. "Everyone needs to be protected from the voice that can kill with one word. His name is Baron Milwr, the son of Lylock."

Ceri speaks to Tim as they wash their hands in one of the fully functional water fountains nearby. "Lylock knows these grounds are his grounds, for Troia Nova only thrives in Selwyn's Chancer because you are here. Even though they are great attackers, they aren't the best thinkers since they rely on instinct like the animals they are."

Tim looks toward Ceri, for he sees her emotions have completely changed; she can barely sleep through the dark nights.

After a day of horror, everyone inside the palace, except for the guards at night, try to get some sleep. Tim is still up, in front of the fire. He's looking at Adamanthea's rope, feeling the power as light circulates throughout his room. On the other side of the palace, Brutus lies in his bed with his arms stretched out. He slowly begins to fall asleep with his sword lying next to him. In Brutus' dream, he watches the Trojan War take place to Achilles death. Images of the past pass before him. His grandfather, Aeneas, carries the Sword of Troy from the burning walls of Troy. He also has dreams of the future in which he creates one of the biggest cities in all the world.

Brutus tosses and turns all night. In an instant, Goddess Diana floats through the window as the white sheer curtains react to her beautiful presence. Diana glances down at Brutus, kissing him on his forehead.

In an instant he falls asleep. Finally at rest. Brutus' mind is in tune with the universe. Diana has given him peace of mind.

On the other side of the palace, Tim sleeps. The night is windy and there are thunderstorms on the horizon. Tim dreams of his friends at Greenhill School, especially Owen, his best friend. Tim dreams about summertime in Tenby and swimming underwater like a fish to see the SS *Walter L M Russ* that he saw Stratford pull out of the water at Grassholm Island. Tim begins to miss the ordinary things in his life that he dreams about. He especially misses the person who matters most: his mother, Mary.

Out of nowhere, the 4th Galon begins to spread its colors of light around the room. The magical power of the Galon begins to effect his dreams. He is now on the south bank of the River Thames but in the twenty-first century. Directly across the river is city hall with its oval-shaped structure. Tim's mind continues to flash images of him running on Tower Bridge. The flashing images zero in on a couple walking on the bridge with 35mm cameras in their hands. Tim hears them speaking, especially the man, who is whispering to a tall woman with blond hair. The man, who is about her size, begins talking about plans to make his Selwyn's Chancer spell take over the world.

As cars pass by, the couple continues to explore more of the bridge, taking pictures as people run across, getting some exercise. Tim notices a cop walking toward him, patrolling the bridge. Tim sees the woman open her long fur coat and pull out a letter as she points toward the river with a massive diamond on her ring finger.

The man pulls out a lighter and places it on the tip of the cigarette he took from his pocket. He pats his brunette hair that is slicked back. He is a true businessman wearing oxford shoes purchased on St. James Street.

The sound of the Thames River fills Tim's ears. The vision in his dream changes to the man leaning over to the woman and saying "Firewyn" three times in a row on the Tower Bridge.

Day turns into night as fast as a Hartwell llwynog (Welsh: llwynog/fox) when Tim snaps out of his dream in a cold sweat, finding himself back in Troia Nova's palace.

He is completely out of strength and silently falls back to sleep as if nothing ever happened moments ago.

Brutus wakes as dawn breaks. He sits at his desk in his personal quarters, thinking about how Ceri's funeral games didn't happen. He thinks about the magical Galon Tim carries along with the Book of Hartwell and the newly found Adamanthea rope. Brutus remains there thinking, and he feels cured in some way. He wonders why the stress in his life has been completely taken away. He stands up and looks at the sun glowing along the horizon. Brutus whispers "City of London" to himself, smiling toward the sun, thinking about his sons, Troia Nova, his grandfather Aeneas, and how discovering new land can manifest into something very magical itself.

All is quiet in the morning in Troia Nova. Men have been lost without warning. Ceri is silently asleep in her bed at the palace. Her heart is broken, shattered into a million pieces for being the last one alive from the House of Gwynwell. Her emotions remain the same, knowing she can not change the past no matter what she does. Nothing can bring back her family, she thinks, lying in her large royal bed.

The sheer drapes over the windows glide from side to side. Black smoke creeps into Ceri's room without her knowing. As she wakes, the smoke begins to turn into a male figure. It's Stratford Hartwell, to be exact. He appears in human form, but his eyes look like those of a panther and he has razor-sharp teeth.

"I could easily end your bloodline with a snap of my finger," Stratford says to Ceri, who has her hood over her face. "Join me, Ceri!" Stratford puts out his hand with his palm facing up. His nails extend all the way down to her hood. He tries to pull it off, for he has never seen her face. Ceri slides out of bed and does a flip to the bed near the balcony. "Don't run, Ceri. Amelia is right behind you, so please, let's talk. Or if you choose not to, you will die before anyone can save you. I won't give you another choice."

Stratford retracts his long nails and sharp teeth, morphing back to normal. Ceri, who had turned to see Amelia, now looks directly at Stratford's face. His face glows like that of Achilles, and he puts Ceri in a trance with his glowing panther-like eyes.

Amelia comes behind Ceri and bites her neck like a vampire, injecting Ceri with her blood. Once penetrated, Amelia's blood will become two separate things: a love potion and a spell for tracking her location in Selwyn's Chancer. Ceri jerks back in unbelievable pain, screaming at the top of her lungs with her voice reaching the sky. At this very moment, no one has heard her cries in all of Troia Nova, except for one person.

Back on the other side of the palace, Tim hears Ceri screaming. He throws on his clothes and runs to Ceri's room where he sees blood coming from her neck. Tim looks up and sees Stratford and Amelia standing on the balcony near Ceri. Tim screams "Firewyn!" to ignite the magical light-blue flame. He blasts his power toward Stratford, but it instantly disappears in a Stairwell of Travel. No one in the palace knows what is going on, for Stratford used the power of Selwyn's Chancer to keep anyone in Troia Nova from knowing where he, Amelia, Tim, and Ceri are.

Tim bends down and wraps his arms

around Ceri, who is on the floor. Amelia's blood mixes with Ceri's. Tim, unaware of what just happened, screams for help, but no one comes. The royal guards are standing outside, but they're unaware of what's going on inside Ceri's room.

Stratford and Amelia travel back into Ceri's room using a Stairwell of Travel. Amelia uses her witchcraft to keep Stratford and herself invisible to Tim and Ceri.

"Let's see you try to escape Selwyn's Chancer now, my dear boy," says Stratford. "Give me the Book of Hartwell and I will end this war against you!"

Amelia steps near the door of the room without Tim or Ceri knowing. The Goddess of Diana has crossed out the power of Selwyn's Chancer for Brutus of Troy, who is holding his sword with the thought of rushing over to Ceri's voice. Brutus walks into the room and only sees Tim holding Ceri on the floor. Brutus raises his sword to see in its reflection Stratford and Amelia standing near Tim and Ceri. Brutus throws his sword, which is aimed directly at Stratford's head. The blade goes right past his ear. Stratford turns toward Brutus, who is amazed that he was hit by a mortal man. Brutus grabs a special dagger from behind him to throw as Amelia's magic once again gets them far away, back to their palace inside of their Alynn dragon.

"What the hell...?" Brutus says with disbelief, turning his head toward Tim who is holding Ceri in his arms. They are all shocked, wondering why Troia Nova wasn't protected.

Tim goes back to normal, as people are still asleep. The guards in the royal halls wake up from a trance. Tim looks at Ceri's skin as it turns back to normal after being pale. Brutus yells out for Procter to come aid Ceri. Procter rushes from his personal chambers, down the royal hallway into her room, looking over Ceri's vital signs.

"I will heal your wounds for you," Procter says, wiping the blood from her neck. He doesn't find any scars or punctures, for they have healed.

Albanactus comes into the room with his two brothers and a few extra guards to watch the door while the three brothers try to figure out the next plan of action and defensive strategies.

As night falls, the people of Troia Nova have high stress levels, for their sacred walls have finally been breached. Tim becomes enraged, and he runs like blazes out of the room using the power of the Galon to run faster than the wind to the Temple of Diana. Tim runs behind some bushes as he stays hidden from the royal guards in front of the temple. He picks up a small stone and tosses it near the guards at the back of the temple. Both guards, without hesitation, run to see what's going on.

Tim runs fast, burning some grass in his trail as he runs inside the Temple of Diana. He walks normal speed when passing the pool and tugs on the lever that opened the secret passage below. He walks in then immediately closes the sliding door behind him using a lever inside the passageway. Tim walks down into the passage, which opens to where he initially met Diana, only this time he doesn't see her by the pool. Diana is nowhere to be found. The torches are still burning, and the sound of pool water hits the inside of the pool walls. Tim screams out, demanding her attention.

"Diana!!!"

Tim continues to scream the same word over and over and then speaks with rage. "There's no reason to hide now, Diana. Show yourself. Aren't you a goddess of the heavens? What are you afraid of?" Tim speaks with a very nasty tone. "Why did I even listen to your words? Why did I have to go through such misery?" Tim opens his heart, wanting to hear the truth. "If Stratford wants the Book of Hartwell, I will give it to him myself." Tim goes way across the line with that particular remark with uncertainty.

"I would be very careful with the words you choose, my dear Tim Hartwell. I think we can both see that the Galon has taken over your emotions," Diana says with a firm tone. She is still invisible.

Another voice begins to speak, catching Tim off guard since he hasn't heard this voice in a while.

"Listen to Diana, Tim," Eleanor Hartwell speaks from the 7th Galon key, which dangles from Tim's neck. The rest of the Galon is forged inside his body. Tim has now become the Galon himself. He has become the key even with anger in his heart.

A young woman's figure made from

water morphs into the goddess Diana wearing a teal-colored dress. Diana only shows because she knows Tim is under the magic of the Galon. She reveals her human self, but she remains on the other side of the pool near the shadows.

"I am hurt by the words you have spoken. All men have choices to make," says Diana. "It's how you deal with those choices that make the big difference. Remember when I told you to trust your heart? I meant every word, including Mary's actions for giving you the Galon." Diana lets Tim know the situation is not going to change whether he likes it or not.

Eleanor says her peace as the voice glows from the 7th Galon. She offers another plan of attack. "Diana, I will guide Tim in the

Death of Ages," she says as she gets up and turns around to face Tim from afar.

"Eleanor, your sight and guidance may not be accurate while in the Death of Ages," Diana explains. "Mary's actions in Tenby will create new rules in Stratford's world, for you see, we are not in Wales. We are in Troia Nova." Diana puts her legs back into the pool. "Only a Gwynwell's touch on the Gates of Death will allow them to enter without paying the Tax of Soulsynwn."

Diana pulls some grapes out of the water with her magical power as a loud noise bangs near the entrance of the passage to their location. Candlelight illuminates the inside of the passage and gets brighter, showing the opening to the pool area. Brutus has come back, knowing

Chapter 5: Revenge Is Bittersweet

Tim has come to see Diana. Tim turns around and notices Diana has disappeared, and Eleanor remains dormant, not saying a word. Brutus walks over to Tim and leads him back to the top of the temple.

"I will guide you to the Death of Ages, and you will have to figure out your destiny, Tim, for before all that, all I knew was a calling from the House of Gwynwell," says Brutus, telling Tim why he has come. He was also surprised that Troia Nova has come with him to Selwyn's Chancer. Brutus really knows the best thing for Tim is to face his destiny.

The next few days nothing happened. Peace somehow is restored to the grounds around Troia Nova. As a man who never runs from fear, Brutus keeps his word and orders the continuation of Lancer's funeral games. This time, he keeps them on the grounds of Troia Nova. Brutus also reminds Tim that after the games, he will take him and Ceri to see the House of Scorpus before they go to the Gates of Death.

A beautiful sun is bright in the sky, and the archery games are packed. Ceri uses a bow and arrow and splits one of the arrows down the middle, placing a bullseye in the center. Kamber makes a few bullseyes himself, for he has always enjoyed archery.

Tim sits alongside Brutus during every game. The remaining days include the chariot race, which Albanactus wins. During the javelin games, Ceri wins with her agility and stuns everyone with her performance. Instead of the giant titan race, Brutus decides to have a running match around

Troia Nova. Locrinus and Kamber tie. After the eleventh day of games, Brutus hands out all the prizes in boxes that are covered with gold paper and ribbons. Each box holds a unique secret customized for each specific winner.

Brutus speaks from a podium, announcing the winners. Ceri receives first place for her boxing match and receives a box full of Lancer's clothing that has been woven into a scarf for her. Also in the box is a dress made by Diana. Since Ceri never wears dresses, it also has a hood on it. Ceri begins to laugh with everyone since she knows she never shows her face. She walks back and stands next to Brutus' sons with everyone clapping for her.

Brutus announces that Locrinus won

second place overall after winning first place in the javelin games, third place in boxing, and second place in the archery games. Locrinus walks over to his father and retrieves his box of honor, which includes one of Brutus' helmets that he used in many wars. Brutus then announces that Kamber won third place overall after placing first in boxing, beating Locrinus with a tap out. Kamber received third place in the javelin games and third place in archery. Kamber walks over to his father to retrieve his gift, opening a long golden box that contains Brutus' spear and arrows. Brutus killed his first giant when he traveled to his new Troy.

At sunset on the twelfth day, Brutus knows he must get Tim out of Troia Nova and head toward the Death of Ages. With only a few more hours until the dawn of the thirteenth day, Brutus informs everyone to be on call so he can take Tim to meet someone special before they head out on their long journey ahead.

Meeting with Claudius

Brutus guides Tim into a secret passageway within the walls of the royal palace. The entrance has a narrow passage with a low ceiling. The passage leads to a midsized room with maps covering the walls. Each map is organized with a specific number or letters. Brutus picks up one of the charts, which has never been opened by anyone, including himself. It was originally given to Aeneas' father, Anchises, when they escaped the burning walls of Troy in the dark-blue night.

Brutus rubs his finger over a hardened Claudius' wax seal.

"How . . . how did Anchises get a scroll from Roman history?" Tim says quickly, looking at the Julio-Claudian dynasty seal holding the chart together.

"We are all part of the royal Crystal Dynasty," Brutus replies while he breaks Claudius' seal on the chart and rolls out the scroll for Tim to check out. Tim scratches his head, for he has never heard of the Crystal Dynasty before. Tim glances down and notices that Brutus has something he never should have known about. Tim remembers reading some of *The Aeneid* by Virgil and understands Aeneas had a shield that told the future of his people.

Brutus, along with Tim, hears a sound that seems so far away. It is the sound of a crowd screaming the name of a Roman emperor who was born into the Julio-Claudian dynasty.

"His full name is Claudius, a name of power," Brutus says as he pulls some red crystals from the drawer built into the wall. Brutus puts nine crystals inside the leather sack on his waist. He then pours a few crystals onto a table as they roll in a diamond shape on the side of the chart. The nine red crystals appear to break apart, turning into a pile of crystal dust on the table. Brutus' eyes shimmer as he reaches over, grabbing some of the crystal dust and pouring it over Claudius' name on the Julio-Claudian dynasty family tree chart.

"I want you to meet someone special to me, " Brutus says. A red-golden light begins to flash throughout the room.

Before Tim even notices what's going on, both of them are transported to the northern area of Campus Martius, directly in front of the huge tomb, the Mausoleum of Augustus. Its stone walls with square travertine shapes for extra support were originally built by Roman emperor Gaius Julius Caesar Augustus in 28 BC.

"If anyone can help you get the proper armor to stay alive in Selwyn's Chancer, he is the person to speak with," Brutus says to Tim. Tim notices they are in the future in his own time of the early 21st century.

Tim begins walking into the huge

entryway leading into the vaulted corridor that leads to the burial chamber. Dust falls from the sides and the ancient walls. Some of the dust travels up Tim's nose, making him sneeze. "The massive size of the tomb looks pretty intimidating," Tim says.

Brutus turns his head, panning the central burial chamber while awaiting the arrival of his mystery guest. Tim begins to wrap the cloth that Brutus gave him even tighter around his wrist, for he begins to ponder the words of Goddess Diana.

Brutus pulls out a few more of the red crystals he brought with him from Troia Nova. He drops the crystals on the floor. They begin to illuminate and float near the ceiling of the chamber, traveling to the corner and gathering into a small niche. The red crystals give off a high-pitched sound when Brutus and Tim walk toward the niche. The sound stops abruptly when the stone surfaces and moves behind the enclosed hatch. A raspy but clear voice speaks to Brutus.

"Who . . . who has disturbed me from my eternal resting place? Who dares to use the power of the red crystals to wake my soul once more?"

"I am looking for Tiberius Claudius Caesar Augustus Germanicus," Brutus says with hesitation. "I am Brutus of Troy. I have used the sacred red crystals you forged during rule to travel time."

"Brutus? Brutus of Troy?" Claudius is shocked to hear the voice of the descendant of Prince Aeneas.

"Yes, Claudius. I have come to you to

help a boy in need. Please tell me, where exactly is the Shield of Aeneas?"

"The Shield of Aeneas, you say?" Claudius replies. "You ask of a priceless item from both of our families' treasures. Would Venus agree to give you such power?"

The magical power of the 5th Galon makes Tim's arms ignite using his Firewyn spell without him controlling it. Tim quickly thinks about Llangollen Bridge, where he obtained such power, when yellow-orange light fills the inside of the central burial chamber. Claudius is not alive but not dead. His spirit comes alive for a short period by the power of the red crystals Brutus brought inside the Mausoleum of Augustus. Claudius can feel the power of the Galon traveling throughout the chamber. Tim turns around, hearing some movements from inside.

Moments later, another voice comes from within the Mausoleum of Augustus. It is that of Livia, third wife of Emperor Augustus and mother of Claudius. Livia's voice echoes throughout the chamber from which they stand guard.

"He who carries the red crystals must be an honorable ancestor of Prince Aeneas of Troy." Livia begins to warm up to her guest, for she knows this must be Brutus of Troy. In honor of her son, Livia convinces Claudius to receive a gift in return before giving away the Shield of Aeneas.

"Brutus, you have heard Livia. What do you have to offer me? I am . . . I am waiting with anticipation," Claudius stutters.

"Claudius, I offer you the rope of

Adamanthea," Tim says as Brutus grabs Tim's wrist, shaking his head for him not to give up something that will help him escape the Death of Ages, even though the Shield of Aeneas could be useful. Brutus changes his mind and lets go of Tim's wrist so Tim can choose his own destiny.

"Adamanthea's rope, you say? Who is the voice that speaks to me, offering such a treasure from Zeus, or should I say, Jupiter?" Claudius says without stuttering this time.

"I am Tim Hartwell, a wizard and descendant of the House of Hartwell. I offer you the rope of Adamanthea for the Shield of Aeneas." Tim repeats what he said earlier but with a more subtle voice hoping Claudius agrees.

Out of nowhere, Verlock and Alfred arrive but remain hidden to the naked eye as they watch the conversation Tim and Brutus are having with Claudius. Alfred whispers a few words to Verlock. "Who would have known that time travel existed in the past from Trojan descendants?"

"He's completely hatstand," says Verlock. "Tim will never get out of the Death of Ages. He better hope he doesn't get caught. I wonder if Claudius will accept their proposal?" Verlock's claw rests on the side of the wall.

"Brutus, you must have trained your pupil well, for the son of Hartwell knows how to offer an emperor like myself such a priceless gift of fortune. I will accept your offer. You may obtain the Shield of Aeneas, which I have kept within these chamber walls, away from humanity. Even after the sack of Rome by the Alarics and when they spilled the ashes of my family and ravaged these vaults, they still did not find your grandfather's most precious gift of all, Brutus."

Claudius makes himself appear as a glowing image behind Tim, catching Tim off guard. Brutus smiles as he and Claudius give each other proper respect and recognition for seeing each other for the first time in ages. Claudius is wearing the proper clothing of an emperor from his reign. He grips Adamanthea's rope with his right hand, which is given to him by Tim. Claudius walks toward another niche inside the ancient burial chamber.

Brutus and Tim follow Claudius' spirit as they pass an invisible Verlock and Alfred inside the burial chamber. Claudius stops in front of the vault of his son, Britannicus. Claudius quickly presses his left hand over the front of the niche, which opens the vault chamber, only to see a vase on a mantle with the ashes of his dear son inside. Claudius looks toward the vase, picking it up for a second then setting it back down. Claudius reaches over to the back wall inside Britannicus' vault, puts his hand inside and twists his wrist left, right, and left twice in a row. The deep sound of a boulder crashing echoes inside the vaulted circular corridor. A large rectangular stone slab built into the wall has fallen onto the stone floor, making dust fly throughout the chamber.

When the dust clears, Brutus and Tim watch Claudius walk to the large stone slab, his head twitching a few times, for he was born with a limp and his head snaps with his disorder, even after death.

Claudius reaches inside the stone slab, pulling out a shield slightly covered with a Roman blanket with Venus' picture on it. Claudius tosses the shield to Brutus so he can hand it to Tim. Brutus nods toward Claudius as he moves slowly back to his resting place inside the central burial chamber. Claudius speaks before his guests from the future and past take off.

"Remember, young boy, that the shield has many magical powers. The future was written on the Shield of Aeneas way before you were born, way back in the time of Brutus' grandfather coming to the shores of Latium. Augustus was very pleased to have Virgil read him *The Aeneid*.

"Brutus, will you promise to come again and tell me more about the streets of Troy? You will be rewarded for your travel if you do."

"I will. The Crystal Dynasty will forge again, Claudius," Brutus replies as he and Tim make their way toward the exit. Tim unravels the blanket from around the Shield of Aeneas before they leave. Tim notices there are four elements that make up the shield. He rubs his fingers along the shield body, touching the engravings of the future of Rome and the creation of the universe on the face of the legendary shield.

"This shield will protect you from the

fires of the Death of Ages, even though you traded Adamanthea's rope," says Brutus, who's seeing the shield for the first time. "Both of them have similarities, one of them being the earth, sky, and sea. Vulcan forged the shield for Venus by her request so she could give it to Aeneas. You will be protected against any power trying to stop you, for not even the strongest magic can penetrate my grandfather's shield. Keep in your mind honor and loyalty, and amazing things will happen for you in the future."

Brutus has flashes in his head of his grandfather fighting the Greeks as they attack Troy, as well as flashes of Aeneas fighting Achilles before almost being killed by him. Tim and Brutus walk out to the gate, which blocks anyone from entering the Mausoleum of Augustus. Brutus pulls out another red crystal from his pouch as they walk closer to the front gates. Brutus tosses the crystals into the air, and they explode like fireworks in the dark night sky. Magical dust falls from the air above onto their bodies, sending them both back to the secret vault room in Troia Nova with the charts and maps.

Before they leave, Brutus picks up one of the maps tucked underneath a few scrolls. He walks back out of the secret room into the royal hallway and behind the large lion statue. Kamber notices them coming out and walks over to them. Respecting their privacy, he doesn't ask about their whereabouts. Brutus tells his son to get his brothers and a few soldiers and meet back in the dining hall for a feast. They will go over the plans of travel to the House of Scorpus near the gates of the Death of Ages.

About half an hour passes, and everyone has eaten well. Brutus picks up his cup and makes a toast before they head off for travel. "Hear me now. Hear my words, my sons, my royal family. I will keep my promise to Diana and Lancer by guiding Tim and Ceri to the Death of Ages. Let's wish them both a safe passage through the depths of Selwyn's Chancer."

Brutus walks beside the long table, surrounded by his comrades. "I have traveled along the oceans. I envisioned a land in my dreams at the very foot of Goddess Diana at her abandoned temple when we arrived."

Everyone begins to smile, since they all love King Brutus and what he stands for. Locrinus gives his final farewell to Tim and Ceri as well.

"It was indeed a pleasure to meet you. I will pray to the gods you will return safely to your home, Tim." Kamber and Albanactus nod their heads in respect.

Everyone at the table stands as Brutus, Tim, and Ceri gather their things to head out. Albanactus glances toward the Shield of Aeneas as Tim picks it up, still inside the cloth. Albanactus' eyes are struck with sight of the shield. Procter rubs his chin, looking at the shield too. Locrinus quickly shouts, "We believe in you."

Albanactus speaks to Tim; Ceri looks at everyone smiling and waving as they head out of the royal palace. Tim, Ceri, and Brutus jump onto their horses to make the long trip toward Snowdonia in Gwynedd.

Brutus tells them to pack everything tightly on their horses, for they never know if they might meet some unexpected guests along the way.

Days turn into dark nights as they travel faster than an arrow shot by Apollo toward North Wales. Along the way, Tim uses his Firewyn spell to ignite one of his hands to light one of the torches he brought to illuminate the land during night travel. Tim ignites another torch, handing it to Brutus and then lights one for Ceri.

"So, where are the gates in the Death of Ages?" Tim asks.

Brutus looks up at the sky as he turns

toward Tim and Ceri to explain. "The House of Scorpus thrives near the Snowdon Massif, near the lake of Llyn Cwellyn toward the east. The castle only appears near the Llyn Cwellyn and Mynydd Mawr at twilight. The Gates of Death are underneath the castle. The only thing in our way is the water that allows you to travel there. At twilight, the ferryman, Charun, will take us to the castle of the House of Scorpus. We must hurry toward the reservoir to make it in time. Let's get there to reach Charun before the end of twilight over Llyn Cwellyn."

They continue to rise along the grounds of Llyn Dinas, passing Llyn Gwynant. Toward the left, they notice Crib Goch, the same arête they walked down the first time they met one another. Ceri begins to ponder why Lancer never mentioned the secret location of the House of Scorpus would be near we he thought the House of Cynfor would be located. But apparently, the leaders of Cynfor has taken their castle down into the Death of Ages.

As twilight approaches, they hear the sounds of large beasts coming toward Llyn Cwellyn from the direction of the Glyderau Range. Brutus, Tim, and Ceri jump off their horses and they quickly gather their weapons. Ceri watches Brutus pull out a beautiful wooden dial with triangle-shaped carvings on the top. The sounds of beasts begin to get louder. Brutus, Tim, and Ceri know they do not have much time to get on the ferry with Charun before the armies from the House of Diablo Arches on their black horses reach their location.

Brutus kneels down and spins the wooden dial on the water, which hovers over the water at Llyn Cwellyn. An ancient horn on Charun's ferry blasts sonic waves that reach as high as the skies. Tim looks behind them and notices thousands of beasts approaching, guided by the House of Diablo Arches, with revenge on their minds. A ferry arrives through the mist toward the end of the reservoir. Brutus tosses three golden coins toward Charun, who grabs them with his half-decayed hands, putting them inside the pocket of his black shredded robe.

Charun moves his hand in a gesture to let them know they have paid their price and may enter the ferry that he only uses on the Llyn Cwellyn. They jump onto the ferry with some of the bones that make up his ferry begin cracking but standing strong. Charun, using his oar, moves them at a decent pace toward the other end of the reservoir. Brutus howls to scare off the horses so the animals won't be murdered by the beasts that approach the Llyn Cwellyn.

The ferry glides halfway across the reservoir as the beasts make their way to the water. Baron Milwr and Lylock look on with disgust, for they missed their chance once again. Tim looks toward Lylock, whose eyes are glaring in the night, along with the eyes of his son, Baron Milwr. Ceri notices Lylock is wearing a Emosiwn Melyn diamond coronet, which illuminates the ground they are standing on, even under the dark night.

Ceri reaches in her pouch and gives Brutus and Tim two Emosiwn diamonds to put next to their ears so they can be protected. They all cover their eyes when Baron Milwr screams out a killing note that shatters the ears of some of the House of Scorpus. The beasts standing next to them without their diamonds fall to the ground, dead. With luck, the House of Scorpus' castle appears near the base of Mynydd Mawr where it meets the Llyn Cwellyn. The howling of Baron Milwr begins to fade away when twilight, at its peak, opens a hidden pocket within Selwyn's Chancer between the Mynydd Mawr and Llyn Cwellyn.

The mist begins to clear as they notice the same mountain hidden in a layer of the parallel world of Selwyn's Chancer. They see a massive stone castle with a wooden gate that goes down into the water. The gate begins to lift when Scorpus' guards notice Charun holding up his left hand with a pendant dangling from a silver necklace. Tim looks on both sides of the ferry, which has bones from some of the House of Diablo Arches who misbehaved. Those stubborn devils. They never learn.

With his mind, Charun moves the six oars inside the ferry. The only treasures he keeps inside are the spirits that bribe him to cross any of the rivers in Selwyn's Chancer, including the Gaia that humans and the river Styx in the underworld.

Large crackling sounds fill the air as Brutus notices guards with human-looking bodies and large scorpion tails waiting for them at the other end of the rigid tunnel leading into the royal Scorpus inner ward.

Guards from the battlements above appear with arrows pointing toward them. There is a west and east tower with fire torches burning high into the night sky.

The eleven-foot Scorpus guards **(eleven feet = 3.3528 meters)** have eight legs. Their claws fit between their elbows and wrists, but they have human hands. Their tails with their stingers spread out along the inner ward stretching twenty-eight feet **(twenty-eight feet = 8.5344 meters)**. Their stingers are deadly. A spirit with direct knowledge of Selwyn's Chancer cannot deny that.

"Scorpus exoskeleton bodies always make a crackling sound, always move in perfect unison," Brutus whispers to Tim. Ceri holds onto Tim's hand when a larger defensive guard from the east tower begins to blow an alphorn, sending a T. Rex roaring sound across the sky. The guard blows on a weird-looking conical bore instrument that they push their wind through. Only Scorpus blood can dilute the poisonous reeds on the instrument that make such a distinct prehistoric sound.

Charun parks the ferry near the docking station. Ceri turns her hooded head toward one of the guards, which makes the Scorpus guard a bit nervous. He growls at Ceri.

"Ceri don't look into his eyes. He will kill you, even if I know his rulers," Brutus says as she grips Tim's hand a little tighter. Tim notices Ceri has changed since the death of her loved ones.

Ceri looks toward the castle, which has long banners draped with the House of Scorpus coat of arms on them. All of the guards have the Scorpus coat of arms on their body armor and weaponry, which shine like their exoskeleton bodies.

Eight Scorpus guards have helmets over their eyes. Their long spears have millions of small stinger needles covering the spear, except for the leather handle that was added as a grip. Four of the Scorpus guards escort them into the castle while the other four break away in formation. Tim looks down at two of the guards' hands. One hand looks human, and the other has a large scorpion claw that can snap any object in two.

The Scorpus guards enter the castle and head into Stywyn Hall and then into the Hall of Judgement where the rulers Darryn & Darron await their guests. Tim begins to ponder the location of the Death of Ages. "It must be around here somewhere," Tim whispers to himself. He looks at the silver railings and massive Emosiwn Melyn diamond chandeliers above them in the middle of the Hall of Judgement.

A lead defensive Scorpus guard greets them in the *Hall of Judgement* and, being a bit nosey, looks at the shield Tim is carrying. Tim switches the shield to his other arm while the guard makes a chomping sound, since he wasn't able to get a better look at what type of shield Tim was carrying.

Darryn & Darron are sitting in two oversized chairs that allow their tails to go through so they can sit in human form. Their twenty-eight councilmen watch from both sides as Tim, Brutus, and Ceri walk down the carpet to the other end of the hall. Darryn, the most outspoken, taps his scepter to the ground like a judge in a courtroom.

"Oh, my brother, do you see what we have here? A hero from Troy and a hero to London. Do I also see a boy Hartwell descendant? What mother has broken the rules in Selwyn's Chancer?" Darryn can't believe Brutus of Troy and the carrier of the magical Galon is right before their eyes. "We can truly believe our eyes, brother, for we must believe our eyes." Darryn has a slight mental problem, which makes him unable to remember who people are. But he never forgets someone who screws him over.

While tensions begin to rise for a second, Darron, the smartest of the two, welcomes his guests properly, for he knows them well, he thinks.

"Brutus of Troy, welcome. Please excuse my brother for his minor sense of humor and memory loss." Darron makes his guests laugh a little while Darryn's head swings back and forth. Darryn's ego makes him arrogant, and he wears a massive Emosiwn Melyn diamond on his hand that once belonged to their original ruler, Hynwyn Reese. Darryn trapped Reese in the Death of Ages when Reese took control of how many spirits he would let through. Darryn's payment was huge amounts of Emosiwn Melyn diamonds from the rich lost souls who weren't granted access to entrance of the Gates of Death.

"Guards, you may stand down, for these are our guests," Darron says, looking over to his defensive general. Darron waves his hand for them to walk out of the Hall of Judgement, except for his personal royal Scorpus councilmen. "You must have traveled a long way here, even though we know you wouldn't be here if someone weren't trying to get into the Death of Ages." Darron looks toward Ceri and Tim, trying to recognize them.

Darryn notices the Coat of Hartwell on Tim's messenger bag and immediately rubs his jagged hands with much excitement.

"Anyone who can make Stratford's words of rage travel across the lands of Selwyn's Chancer may speak to me anytime he wants."

Darron laughs, for he doesn't like Stratford too much himself. "Speak, my boy. Let me hear the voice of the boy who killed the ruler of the House of Cynfor.

"My name is Tim Hartwell, son of Mary, member of the House of Hartwell. This is my friend, Ceri, from the House of Gwynwell." Tim is not afraid of their ridged bodies as they look at young Ceri with her hood up.

"This might call for a celebration. A Hartwell, a Gwynwell and a Trojan. I must be dreaming," Darryn says, adding more humor. Brutus remains unfazed as Tim begins to speak again.

"Darron & Darryn, your excellencies, we are here for the drink of the gwenwyna."

"Gwenwyna you ask for, dear boy? We apologize, for we only have a fraction left. It won't be enough for you three, only two of you," Darryn lies while keeping a disappointed look on his face.

"I will not be heading with them, you see," says Brutus. "I am here to do a favor for an old friend who has passed."

"Death of a friend, you say?" Darron says with some concern. "I will grant you two glasses of gwenwyna, even though I know my councilmen won't agree with anyone undead traveling there, for only the dead of Selwyn's Chancer live there. But . . ." Darron stands up, along with his brother. "It will take approximately six hours for their bodies to heal from the effect of gwenwyna. While their bodies rest, I will show you how to get back to Troia Nova without being seen from the House of Diablo Arches."

"No need, but thank you, for the goddess Diana will lead me home," Brutus says as Darron's face looks weird with his eyes bugging out a bit.

"No apology needed, for if Goddess Diana is around, we know you will be safe," Darron replies. "After they drink the gwenwyna, I will show them the hoist in the *West Tower*. It leads to the Death of Ages. Follow us to the *Chamber of Gwenwyna*. We will have to strap their bodies onto the beds to keep them from killing themselves. Unbearable pain is a side effect for humans who drink gwenwyna because the poison runs through their veins. But they will survive."

Darryn waves for their councilmen to ready the Chamber of Gwenwyna at once.

The Scorpus rulers, along with Brutus, Ceri, and Tim, head toward the Great Hall that leads to the opposite end of the Chamber of Gwenwyna. Darron begins to speak about a few things none of them might of heard about the Death of Ages.

"I hope you are fast on your feet. Members of the House of Cynfor are growing to the size of titans down there, and only their lungs can breathe the air," he says looking at Tim.

"Stratford will know you are there once Tim steps on his most precious land. The House of Cynfor won't expect to meet such a powerful wizard as yourself, I might add. We have heard about your victory in defeating the powerful Miniver and Cynhafar."

They pass many rooms with different symbols covering each door. Darryn & Darron notice that Tim is carrying a shield, but they don't recognize it as the Shield of Aeneas. They continue down the Great Hall, which leads to arched metal doors with a large metal locking system. The Coat of Scorpus is forged onto the top of the door. Darron unlocks the door with a special sequence of metal buttons. Darryn looks toward Ceri, still trying to figure out what her face looks like beneath her hood.

"She must be one of the ugliest girls in all of Selwyn's Chancer," Darryn says.

"Excuse my brother. He must watch

his tongue," Darron says.

"I didn't know scorpions have tongues," Ceri says, giving some humor back.

"Feisty little one, I see, Brutus. She must be the daughter of Henry Gwynwell to speak the way she does," says Darron.

"You knew my father?" Ceri asks.

"We didn't know your father, but we know where his spirit is located," says Darron. "Henry is locked in the dungeon of Bledri and Tomes, we have heard from some of the bribers coming our way. You would be surprised what you can learn from someone who hasn't been given approval to enter the Gates of Death."

"We must find my father at once!" Ceri demands as she looks toward Tim. "That means Lancer must be there as well," she adds as she loses it for a moment, thinking she can see her beloved again.

"Yes, but you cannot save them now, for they are already locked in a horrid place," says Darron. "The only person who can free them is Stratford. Just don't make a deal with anyone in the Death of Ages. Stratford knows everything." Darron stops talking as he leads them into the Chamber of Gwenwyna.

The Scorpus councilmen appear wearing navy-blue robes with yellow trim and the Coat of Scorpus on their chest, which they wear proudly. Each councilmen is holding a candle as he faces two stone slabs, which look like beds. Darron points toward the slabs, which are for Ceri and Tim to lie upon for the gwenwyna process.

Dawn breaks as the sun's rays sneak from behind the walls to shine through the stained glass depicting the fallen kings through the ages of the House of Scorpus. Tim and Ceri walk near the beds and lay their things on the rock slabs.

"Stay strong, you two." Brutus gives words of encouragement as Tim and Ceri lie down, looking at the ceiling of the chamber. Two Scorpus councilmen lay yellow linen over Tim and Ceri, which has Scorpus symbols of witchcraft and wizardry. Darryn & Darron take their royal seats, pointing toward Brutus to join them to watch the ritual of the Gwenwyna.

All twenty-eight councilmen walk into the chamber. Two of them hold a metal platter with two ridged glasses with oval bottoms. The councilmen break out of formation in unison and walk down both red carpets leading to Ceri and Tim. The other twenty-six councilmen begin repeating their words over and over.

"Gwenwyna, gwenwyna"

The Scorpus councilmen yell the name of their poison faster and faster as the cups get nearer and nearer to Tim and Ceri. The councilmen raise the metal platter high in the air, then bring it down in front of them. In mere seconds, the councilmen stop singing, which makes Tim and Ceri a bit nervous. Tim and Ceri grip the stone slabs as the Scorpus councilmen lift the yellow linen sheets over both their heads in unison, then pour the gwenwyna poison directly into their mouths through an opening in the sheet. Four guards walk over to Tim and Ceri; two hold down their arms and legs so they can't get away.

Within a few minutes, Tim and Ceri begin screaming with dreadful pain as the gwenwyna travels throughout their bodies. Their voices echo throughout the chamber. Both Ceri and Tim's eyes begin turning light orange as the gwenwyna poison circulates evenly throughout their system. Ceri screams again, and her voice shatters the crystal cups the guards carried the poison in. Brutus, along with Darron & Darryn, is amazed that her vocal octaves can reach that high. Tim begins screaming along with Ceri, tossing and turning as they try to free their bodies from agony. Tim and Ceri feel like their bodies are being burned alive. Everyone looks on as the gwenwyna poison continues to take effect.

Some unexpected Wyvern guests appear high in the rafters and look down at the entire group in the chamber. It's Verlock and Alfred, the protectors of the Galon and the Book of Hartwell. Both of them remain invisible to the crowd below and keep an eye on them. Otherwise, Stratford will kill them.

"They must be completely hatstand!" Verlock whispers, seeing the pain Tim and Ceri are withstanding could kill any normal human being.

"If Brutus wasn't around, I am sure, Verlock, they both would have been stuck in Selwyn's Chancer forever," Alfred replies as his claw grasps one of the rafters and he jumps to another to get a better look. "Why didn't Stratford destroy the House of Scorpus when he had the chance ages ago? They must have made a deal with him to survive over the ages. If Tim gets inside the gates of the Death of Ages, we will have to protect them, no matter what Stratford thinks."

"Yes, my brother, but Stratford will lock us in Bledri and Tomes' dungeon if we do. I am willing to die for Tim. We cannot be afraid of Stratford or Amelia any longer," says Verlock.

"I am tired of being slaves to them," says Alfred. "We need to be free."

Alfred and his twin jump onto another rafter, then fade into thin air. Just before they disappear, Verlock whispers, "Tim has acquired the Shield of Aeneas. Who would have known it was still inside the Mausoleum of Augustus?"

"Yes, I know," Alfred says, waiting for the right time to come back again. The twin Wyverns are content with each other. Their eyes sparkle as they disappear into another part of the world in Selwyn's Chancer.

Down The Hoist

Brutus, along with the rulers of the House of Scorpus, remains very quiet inside the Chamber of Gwenwyna. Four councilmen who are holding down the arms of Tim and Ceri begin to slowly let go of them in unison. The remaining Scorpus councilmen who are singing begin to slow down, along with the councilmen who are letting go of Tim and Ceri. All of their voices lower while everyone looks at Tim and Ceri lying down. Darryn & Darron are especially curious to see who awakens first.

Brutus' eyes are slim as he looks toward Tim, who is beginning to move around, groaning from the pain he withstood. Tim leans up from beneath the sheets, using his right hand to pull them off. His eyes turn from light orange back to their normal brown color. Tim swings his legs around the edge of the stone slab and rubs his hand over his head, trying to get his senses back to normal again.

Ceri starts moving around beneath her sheet. Her hood almost slips, revealing her face, but with a quick reaction, she pulls it back down to keep her identity a secret. Brutus steps forward to make sure they are all right. Darron warns Brutus to wait until the effects of the poison completely wear off Ceri. Brutus takes one step to the side when Ceri gets off the stone slab, looking at Tim beginning to collect his things that are still next to the base of the stone slab.

"*Wait!*"

Darron's voice projects throughout the entire chamber. He orders his guards to stop Ceri, for all Scorpus councilmen must see her eyes to make sure the gwenwyna worked correctly.

"The girl must take off her hood and reveal her eyes. Show us your eyes, young girl. We demand that you show your eyes immediately," Darron says with a stern voice but meaning no harm to their guests.

Ceri turns and faces the direction of

Darryn & Darron. "I will show my face to no one. Not you, not anyone, except for the House of Gwynwell. Since you know I am the last one, neither of you will see," Ceri says with a lot of emotion.

Darryn claps his hands together in a particular sequence, which alarms more of the army that storms into the Chamber of Gwenwyna. Brutus unsheathes his sword, putting his blade to Darron's neck, for he believes the royal rulers of the House of Scorpus are up to something.

"Why must the girl reveal her face? Why is it so important for her to reveal herself to you both?" Brutus yelling out.

The Scorpus guards jump fast into position, holding their sharp scepters toward Ceri. Darryn, fearing for his brother's life, explains the reason for the special request.

"If her eyes remain light orange, she will be forced to be the watcher of the Last Fairy Maze Forest in the Death of Ages. She will turn into a fairy who cannot see. Only by movement will she be able to hear. She will trap herself in a forest that never ends, with roads that lead nowhere except right back to the back entrance of the castle."

Ceri's tone changes, for she just might have to reveal her identity after all. Brutus retracts his blade from Darron's neck and sheathes his sword. The Scorpus general defensive and the rest of the guards lower their defenses.

"Ceri, please do as they say. I know how much your identity means to you, but I guess you don't have a choice," Tim says as he calls off his Firewyn spell and the flame extinguishes. Ceri walks between the rock slabs, looking up toward the rulers. Tim walks over to Brutus as they look on, for they have never seen her face. Ceri pulls down her hood, going as slow as possible, for the pressure to show her face is overwhelming for her. As the hood slides back, her beautiful brunette hair is exposed. The entire chamber whispers. The councilmen are shocked to see her eyes with the light-orange color. The councilmen inside the chamber begin to whisper louder when Tim notices something about Ceri that no one else in the chamber sees, except for him.

"Zoe? How can this be?" Tim notices that Ceri is also Zoe Beckham from his Greenhill school.

"Yes, it's me, for I am Zoe Beckham in your world, but my real name is Ceri Gwynwell in Selwyn's Chancer."

Tim almost falls down in shock, knowing that the girl he had a crush on at Greenhill has been helping him on his journey the entire time.

"I have been watching you, Tim," says Ceri. "My family has known about you ever since your birth. I am sorry if you are disappointed in me for not telling you the truth all along."

"You have more problems now than an identity crisis," Darron says. "There is only one person who can stop the transformation of you becoming the sole watcher of the Last Fairy Maze Forest in the Death of Ages."

Darryn, with a serious tone, says, "No

one will be able to free her from the maze."

Darron pauses for a moment to order all of his councilmen and guards out of the chamber at once. They walk out, whispering to themselves, for they know something is up. The guards close the high chamber doors behind them to give their new guests some privacy.

"You both are now physically capable of breathing the air in the Death of Ages. But, we are breaking a bond with Stratford to let you go free, young girl. Only for Brutus have we decided to lead you to the hoist in the West Tower, which will take you down into the earth under Mynydd Mawr to the Death of Ages. Gather your things and come with us immediately," Darron says as his scorpion tail sways back and forth.

Darryn & Darron walk over to the Great Hall, which leads to the West Tower. The walls are covered with battle achievements and skeleton heads as trophies. In the West Tower, there is a wooden door that Darron opens to reveal the hoist attached to a long chain that is connected to the peak of the West Tower. Darron sways his hand toward the hoist for Tim and Ceri to get into.

Brutus looks at both of them inside the hoist and says his farewell, for he knows this might be the last time he ever sees them alive. "Be safe, you two. It was an honor for me to help you along your journey. I will always remember the stories you told me about the lands that I discovered growing into something magical. I will continue to pray for your safety. Remember, Tim, you use the shield well. Trust your heart. Always remember that. Ceri, protect Tim the best you can, for he will find a way to heal you from being the watcher of the maze." Brutus puts his right hand over his heart.

Darron reaches inside his long robe and pulls out a medium-sized canister that contains liquid. "Young girl, this will help slow down the process of your fairy transformation," he says as Ceri grabs the canister and pulls her hood back up, getting ready for what they might face in the depths of Selwyn's Chancer.

"Thank you for caring, even though I know you don't have to," Ceri says as Tim glances over to her with a different look, since he now knows she is Zoe Beckham from Greenhill.

Darron shuts the metal gate to the hoist, pulling a metal switch that makes it descend into the mountain of Mynydd Mawr. Brutus looks down and salutes them.

The metal hoist clanks as it descends into the ground. Tim screams out

"FIREWYN"

This ignites his arms with a light-blue flame so they can see inside the hoist going down the shaft. The air becomes thin as they ride further and further into the earth, both not knowing what to expect next. All of a sudden, a strong gust swoops through the shaft, blowing the edges of their clothes. Tim and Ceri stand guard, for they don't have the slightest clue what to expect during their journey, besides the evil castle of the House of Cynfor.

Ceri pulls off her hood and quickly gives Tim a kiss on the cheek, which catches him off guard.

"What was that for?" Tim says.

"I've never kissed a boy in my life, so if I'm going to die, I might as well kiss someone while I'm still alive," Ceri says, pulling her hood back up.

After a few minutes, the hoist drops faster into the shaft, going thousands of meters inside the earth's crust. Tim and Ceri crouch down, bracing for impact as the hoist continues to descend. They close their eyes, for dust begins to fill the shaft from the speed of the descent. The temperature inside the shaft gets hotter and hotter the further they descend down into the earth.

Without notice, the old hoist begins

to slow down, and a red-toned light illuminates beneath it. The air almost smells like nectar and ambrosia, which are the same substances the gods use to wash and cleanse the sinful flesh of humans before they are reborn. The smell gets stronger and stronger the more they descend. Tim and Ceri look at each other as they begin to hear the sound of a river.

"Is that the sound of water?" Tim says as they stand up.

"I believe so," Ceri says as she ponders how water could be in the depths of Selwyn's Chancer.

The light becomes brighter beneath the shaft. The hoist screeches a bit while it transitions to a stop.

"We must be getting closer to the

end of the shaft!" Tim says loudly as the hoist clanks against the rocky walls of the narrow, dusty shaft.

BOOM!

The hoist slams loudly on the bottom. Tim and Ceri open their eyes as the dust clears, noticing a reddish world in front of them that almost looks like Mars. The powerful River Styx is down a medium-sized hill ahead of them.

"The Death of Ages?" Tim says as they step onto the red sand ground. As they look back, they notice a huge train behind them, and the hoist they rode down on is inside one of the train's cars. Tim and Ceri look up to a dark, blue-toned sky, wondering where the shaft or mountains are. The sky turns from blue to dark orange many times during a day's cycle in the Death of Ages. Tim and Ceri look at the sky, wondering exactly what they've gotten themselves into.

The Gates of Death

The door of the hoist that was behind Tim and Ceri slams shut as the rugged train begins to move again. Tim looks right and notices two beastly figures called Vonixra. One stands more than six meters high. Tim looks up at one of the mysterious characters who wears a long black trench coat that goes all the way down to his large feet. The other Vonixra beast is about three meters tall. They speak to each other in their strong native language.

Vonixras are immortal, and their sole purpose is to control the traffic of dead spirits traveling to the Death of Ages. Both of the beasts are laughing about something, for they haven't even noticed Tim and Ceri looking at them. The taller beast begins to speak in his Vonixrian language.

"Ana Carantoc gugin fulira."

(The Carantoc gladiator games

will be fun to watch later.)

Another train made from old rugged steel moves into place. More dead spirits walk out of the train as its horn blasts into the air. The Vonixras begin pushing the spirits toward the long line of dead spirits gathered along the River Styx down the hill below.

Tim and Ceri wonder why they haven't been noticed. They begin to walk in the opposite direction of the train. Tim uses the power of the 4th Galon to tap Into his vision and look down the hill past hundreds of different beasts gathered at the wooden station of Charun on the river Styx. Tim looks across the river to large gates, which are connected to high-level battlements that travel as far as the eye can see in either direction over the horizon.

"We need to find a way to the other side," Tim says as they continue in the opposite direction of the train.

Ceri notices the air has gotten thicker. "This truly is the River Styx," she says, looking toward the water. "The Styx is wrapped around the earth nine times." She stops speaking as they notice a large black ship crossing the river approaching the Port of Charun. Tim's hearing has improved, and he can now hear the train that dropped them off stopping not too far from their location.

Ceri wonders why they aren't going with the rest of the souls onto the ship, which is docking in the port, for they will never be able to cross the River Styx without the help of Charun.

"I have another idea," says Tim. "Do you see these small pebbles? These will help us get across the dreadful river."

"Well, how and the hell are we going to do that?" Ceri replies as Tim pulls her arm so they can run down the hill and be closer to the river. As they run, Tim notices a section of the River Styx that's smaller than the rest.

"This is the perfect spot," Tim says as he holds the two pebbles in his hand that Brutus had given him. Ceri looks on, wondering what in the world Tim is going to do. Tim plants the pebbles in the sand just like Brutus told him to. In a matter of seconds, the pebbles begin to grow as the sand spreads out into two large oval shapes. In a flash, the shapes drop back into the desert without anything happening.

"I guess they were broken," Tim says lightheartedly. Suddenly, two large horses leap out of the desert with their two front legs high in the air. The horses have saddles on their backs and metal helmets over their heads for protection. The helmets have ancient symbols on them, which were engraved by Jupiter. Their eyes flame with light, and their muscular legs grind into the sand. The horses are trained to immediately obey the individual who planted them. Jupiter's horses stand in front of Tim and Ceri, awaiting their orders.

Down on the other side of the River Styx, some of the dead spirits begin boarding Charun's ferry. Tim uses his vision to once more zero in on Charun with his rugged body and the same torn, sheer robe, except this time, Charun is using the main oar to steer the ship. Charun notices that some of the dead spirits have not been buried properly and are trying to sneak onto the ferry along with the approved spirits. Some of the disrespectful spirits bombard the ferry since they want to wander the sands of the outer regions of the Death of Ages.

One of the outer regions is called Emosiwn, which is where the high-pressure and high-temperature Caves of Siôr are located. They are also the same deep caves where the precious Emosiwn Melyn diamonds are mined.

"In a secret vault, Stratford keeps the largest pink and yellow diamonds from the caves," says Eleanor, speaking from the 7th Galon that appears around Tim's neck. "He deports spirits from the dungeon of Bledri and Tomes to mine at the *Caves of Siôr* for an eternity."

Down near the river, one particular spirit from the House of Diablo Arches, who died in war, is causing a disruption on

Charun's ferry as the spirits fight to board the ship. The lost spirit rips apart some of the other spirits on the ferry with his huge arms and oversized muscles. Charun, having enough of their child's play, begins to throw spirits into the River Styx. The spirits scream for their lives, for they will drown in the river and stay there for an eternity. Their cries reach the skies as they scream for mercy as they are tossed one after another into the river Styx.

Charun begins to laugh as the lost souls drown, for they are completely helpless. Charun grips a scepter that was next to him and screams into the sky as thick black smoke comes out of his mouth. The smoke pours high into the sky then turns into liquid acid as it descends onto all the lost souls who should be crossing on the ferry. The acid eats their spirit bodies until nothing is left, except for their skeleton bodies, which are made of light. All of the approved spirits in the ferry are left unharmed by the acid, which stops descending from the darker blue-orange sky as dusk approaches.

Charun grips his scepter and starts smashing the skeletons, sweeping them into the river as they clank off his ferry and dissolve into the River Styx. Charun, for some reason, starts saving the spirits who were supposed to get a lift and pulls them back into the boat.

"I guess he has a heart after all," Tim says as they continue to watch from afar.

Tim begins to get restless and jumps onto his horse, then tells Ceri to follow his lead by doing the same. Down below, Charun has gotten all the spirits together and is making his way across the river near the Gates of Death, which have long iron beams going up and down. A huge Trydan skull is positioned on the front of the gate for intimidation. That particular Trydan was killed by Bledri and Tomes' lionfaced father, Cynhafar, even though the dragon-headed Miniver always took the credit.

Large, dark, iron and steel ride makes up the top of the gate. Tim notices a moat with slime oozing from the bailey. He and Ceri hear men and women screaming on the other side of the battlements. They look at each other as they wait for the right moment to cross the heavy-flowing River Styx. Moments later, Charun parks his ferry on the other side of the river, pulling an oval handle connected to a rope attached to an ancient bell mounted on the top of the long sacred ferry.

When Charun pulls the handle down harder, two large Cynfor dragons appear on the top of the barbicans, which connect the sides of the Gates of Death. The Cynfor dragons with their two heads look down to make sure everything is safe below so they can open the gates. One of the dragons blows a large horn that produces a loud sound and steam. Tim and Ceri cover their ears as the horn's power makes the water overflow the banks near the Gates of Death. Both of the Cynfor dragons, who are gatekeepers, growl as they open the locking system from the other side of the

Gates of Death.

Four Cynfor dragons push open the gates as the dinosaur skull slides up, allowing the gates to open like suicide doors.

Two Cynfor dragons, who are third in line to the throne, walk out to meet their new batch of fresh spirits that are entering in one line through the Gates of Death. One of the Cynfor's names is Derilyn, and it has a dragon head; the lionface head is named Geulia. The other Cynfor dragon's name is Fyanicrum, and his lionface head is called Jupira. The Cynfor's approach the ship carrying their humongous swords in their hands. The swords are so big they could cut down even the largest dragon in one swipe. Derilyn uses his tail and sticks the large blade into the ground, trying to intimidate the dead spirits of Selwyn's Chancer, for most of them are afraid of any Cynfor.

Some of the spirits used to work for Stratford and Amelia and failed in their duty or were killed in wars orchestrated by the House of Diablo.

Tim looks as Ceri moves her hood back so half of her lower face shows and her eyes can be seen. Tim notices Ceri's eyes are still a light orange color. He wonders whether he will be able to cure her from becoming the watcher of the Last Fairy Maze Forest. Ceri keeps Tim patient while they sit on Jupiter's horses. Tim looks down at the Shield of Aeneas sparkling on the side of his horse. He reaches inside his messenger bag and pulls out the Book of Hartwell. Ceri looks at him, shocked to see such magical power in her presence.

"So, that is the Book of Hartwell. Why haven't you used any of its magical power?" Ceri asks as she continues to watch spirits enter the Gates of Death to the castle of Bledri and Tomes.

"I can't open it," Tim says to Ceri. "I thought once I found all seven Galons I would be able to see what my family has hidden throughout the ages. Even the spells have been written by the book itself, for it has become alive somehow." Tim tucks the book back into his messenger bag, and a place flashes in his mind.

"The Peninsula of Roseland," Tim says to himself, for he knows where he must go to open the Book of Hartwell so he can find a way home. First, he must rescue Ceri from her doom. Second, he must find Hynwyn Reese. And third, they must escape the Death of Ages.

Tim along with Ceri wait for the Cynfor dragons to leave before they go back through the entrance. Fyanicrum screams as the gates shut completely, and no one can hear his screams on the inside. Tim and Ceri continue and ride their horses to the front of the gates of Death. Ceri touches the dinosaur's skull on the gate. Her father's signet ring slowly illuminates on her right hand. The power of her Gwynwell bloodline magically opens the Gates of Death to the House of Cynfor where Bledri and Tomes are secretly awaiting their arrival.

Coat of Brutus

(Worn by Brutus of Troy)

TIM HARTWELL **and The Brutus of Troy**

(Worn by the House of Trydan)

Coat of Diablo Arches

(Worn by the House of Diablo Arches)

TIM HARTWELL and The Brutus of Troy

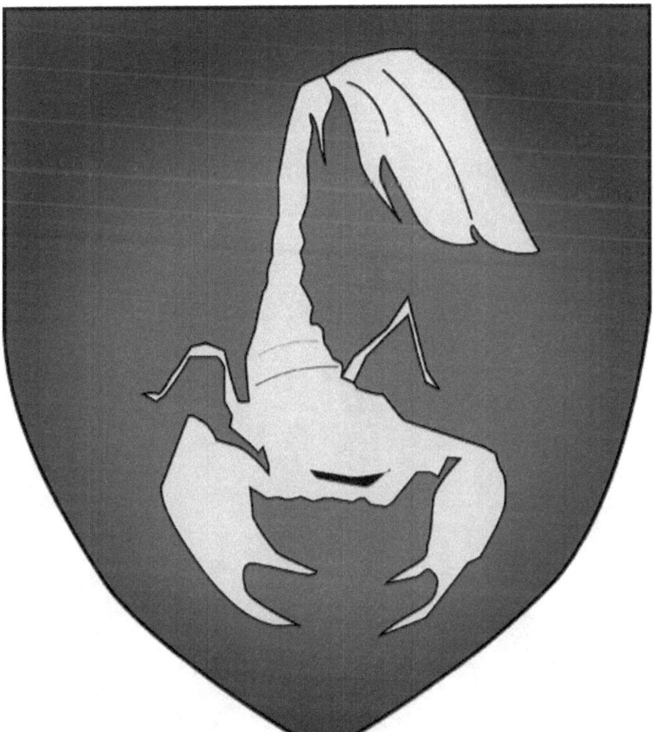

(Worn by the House of Scorpus)

Goddess Diana

Brutus of Troy TIM

Castle to the House of Scorpus

HALL OF JUDGEMENT

CHAMBER
OF GWENWYNA

House of
Scorpus

LLYN CWELLYN RESERVOIR

North Wales

Mynydd Mawr

Snowdon massif

Only at twilight, will the castle of the House of Scorpus appear on the horizon between the reservoir of Llyn Cwellyn and the mountain of Mynydd mawr.

-Brutus of Troy

Llyn Cwellyn

Location: Nant y Betws, Gwynedd, North Wales

Brutus of Troy

A mythological figure who

discovered Great Britain along with

founding the city of London, or Troia

Nova. His grandfather, Aeneas, another

legendary hero from Troy.

Like Brutus, his destiny

leads him to Latium, now called Rome.

TIM HARTWELL and The Brutus of Troy

Arma

virumque

cano

(I sing of arms and of man - *The Aeneid*)